T0106140

KAITO

Shedding Tears

Michelle Y. Richardson

iUniverse, Inc.
New York   Bloomington

Kaito
Shedding Tears

iUniverse books may be ordered through booksellers or by contacting:

iUniverse
1663 Liberty Drive
Bloomington, IN 47403
www.iuniverse.com
1-800-Authors (1-800-288-4677)

Because of the dynamic nature of the Internet, any Web addresses or links contained in this book may have changed since publication and may no longer be valid. The views expressed in this work are solely those of the author and do not necessarily reflect the views of the publisher, and the publisher hereby disclaims any responsibility for them.

ISBN: 978-1-4502-5267-6 (pbk)
ISBN: 978-1-4502-5268-3 (ebk)

Printed in the United States of America

iUniverse rev. date: 11/1/10

CHAPTER ONE

The Shed

Today is the day I have been waiting for. I feel my eyes beginning to open slowly. The light seems so bright at first I have to keep closing them, slowly peaking as I open them again. After what seems to be a long time of opening and closing, they are finally staying open, accepting the daylight. The images I see are somewhat contradictory from what I'd anticipated from the sounds I'd been hearing.

First, I see the fur of my mother. She has soft gray and white fur with muted stripes on the gray. Some of her fur is matted and dirty as we are living under a shed and she does not have much opportunity for grooming herself. She is a on the petite side, which made it difficult for her to deliver my brother, sisters and me.

"Mother?" I questioned, looking directly at her.

"Can you see me?" She asked.

"Yes. But..." I stuttered, unsure how to tell her she wasn't quite what I'd expected.

"But, what? What's the matter? Can't you see me clearly?" She worried.

"Yes! I see perfectly. It's just, well, I thought that everything was going to look different. That's all," I admitted.

"So, what did you expect you'd see?" She prodded, urging me to tell her.

Often, I found my mind unintentionally wandering, conjuring up unexpected and surprising daydreams. Previously, I hadn't revealed to anyone my unusual inclination to create such fantasies. Not sure of what mother's reaction would be, I remained temporarily frozen in silence, hoping she would not ask me again.

With a tender, understanding tone, she delicately said, "You can tell me, whatever it is. After all, I'm your mother."

Nervously, I stammered as I began, "I thought you'd be all white with a long sleek, shiny coat of fur. A bright pink collar would be hanging around your neck, full of sparkling gems. I pictured that you were a pampered, glamorous queen."

Curiously, mother smirked, while I continued to describe to her all that I had envisioned. I pictured my siblings and me sitting upon billowy, satin cushions, trimmed with golden tassels; our home illuminated with a flickering, glowing candlelight, bouncing a variety of colors onto the walls and ceiling from the dazzling gems.

Mother's apparent amusement with my story abruptly broke my concentration. Stopping myself from telling her any more, I suspiciously asked, "Why are you laughing? Aren't you upset that we aren't really royal cats?"

"You have quite an imagination, little one," she said. "Our home is far from a palace. We live in a cold, dirty hole, under a broken down, old shed. My meals are scavenged, not served to me on a silver tray. We lie on a dirt floor, surrounded by bits of trash, barely keeping warm."

With a grim look on her face, she went on, "I'm sorry if you're disappointed by what you see. This is the best that I can do. I can tell you this though. I do love you more than anything a wealthy queen's money could buy."

Aware that I'd offended her, I knew that I had to reassure her that really none of this mattered, for I loved her no matter what.

Rubbing my head onto her chest, I kindly said to her, "Mother, I'm glad that we don't live like that. If we did then I suppose we'd have to keep clean all of the time. What fun would that be? This is so much better. Plus, you are more beautiful than I could have ever imagined in my mind. Everything is perfect. As long as we are together, it doesn't matter where we are!"

Relieved, mother gave me a big cuddle, before turning to attend to the others who were becoming a little restless.

Mother is a young cat, just shy of a year old. We are her very first litter of kittens. There are four of us altogether, two boys and two girls. I am told by my mother that I am an orange tabby. I have stripes just like her with four white paws. My nose is pink with half orange and half white fur. Mom thinks this makes me look special. One of my sisters is a calico and the other is just like mom. My brother, mom says, looks like my dad. He is smaller than I am with a soft brown coat with very distinct black stripes.

It is winter where we live which makes it a little unusual for mom to have had her kittens now. They say that this has been a mild winter, although it feels pretty cold to me. Sometimes there is a draft that blows on us from the opening that mom squeezes out of, making the dirt floor feel even colder. For warmth my siblings and I nestle into one big pile. Often we curl up with mom, who is able to keep us all warm and snuggled. Even though we have to stay under this shed until mom feels it is safe enough to leave, we are all anxious to see what is out there. I am especially curious, and now that I can see, I cannot wait to be allowed to explore. Until then I am content to nuzzle with my siblings and drink my mom's warm milk. She is a good mother who stays with us, protecting us the best she can. Sometimes though, she must go out to find food for herself.

There is a restaurant dumpster, not far from here, where she can find a good meal. Then she comes right back to us. She tells us to stay put until she returns. We always listen to her. Before today, where could we go without being able to see?

My sisters opened their eyes for the first time yesterday and my brother is still awaiting his chance. Perhaps tomorrow will be the day for him. Until then I tell him about all that surrounds us. Describing to him the different colors of our fur, the piercing green eyes of our mother and the old rusty soda cans that have somehow made their way under this decrepit shed, he sits still and listens silently and attentively.

When night falls it is so dark in our little home that it is almost as if my eyes have never opened. I shut them and cuddle up with my sisters, brother, and mother feeling comforted by the familiar sound of the soft purring. She lies quietly with us, always listening to the sounds from the outside. There are many dangers at night for us. This is when many bigger animals awaken and forage for a meal.

Although I haven't ventured outside as of yet, I have dreamt about what awaits us when the time ultimately arrives. Without notice, my thoughts inconspicuously float away, taking me to that make-believe place full of never-ending possibilities.

A gloomy darkness covers all; forming ominous shadows everywhere I look. Shrieking howls in the distance seem to draw closer with each holler. The greatness of the vast outdoors dwarfs my little body drastically, causing me to feel even smaller than I am. Danger seems to lurk in every corner.

My heart pounds faster, thumping with fright. My wobbly legs, quivering, attempt to transport me to safety. Dashing as hurriedly as I am able, I head for refuge. Surely, the vicious predators have detected my scent by now and are steadily closing in. With each step, my legs become heavier and more sluggish, slowing me down.

Crack! Twigs are snapping under their massive footsteps! They must be gaining ground! How am I to outrun the ferocious creatures that stalk the nighttime? Barely capable of movement, I persist with desperately dragging my tired body onward. Glancing back, I can see the outline of their immense figures rapidly approaching. Circling around me like a school of sharks, they move in for the hunt.

Drool dribbles from their jaws as these monsters snarl and growl angrily. Wicked, glowing eyes watch me intently, preparing for the timely attack. Whimpering in terror, I curl up into a ball, covering my eyes so as not to see the first strike from their gnarled, sharp-edged claws. If only I were out of harm's way, beneath the protected shed, safe with mother.

Cringing, I anticipate the blow. Shockingly, I believe instead I hear a voice calling faintly. "Orange tabby! Orange tabby!"

I must be hearing things, I conclude, returning to my state of impending doom. When will these beasts begin their lethal assault? I can't stand the suspense of the terror any longer!

"Orange tabby! Orange tabby!" There was the voice again, only louder this time.

Something touched my shoulder. This was it! I screeched with a shrill in pure panic! Wait! There was no slashing or onslaught to follow. What was touching me?

"Orange tabby!" shouted the voice. It was mother! With a hard shake, I snapped back into reality. She had single-handedly rescued me from my dreadful nightmare.

"Mother?" I cried.

"I could tell by the far away look in your eye that you were off again in some sort of wild daydream," she said.

Catching my breath, the racing of my heart began to slow. "Thank you for saving me from the night creatures! They were about to attack!" I told her.

She rolled her eyes, letting me know she did not want to hear anymore. It was late and I had apparently kept everyone from falling asleep. They were all tired, and understandably a little annoyed with me. Taking the cue, I apologetically snuggled with the group, being careful to keep quiet.

Before long, we all drifted off into a peaceful slumber. One piled on top of another, so close that even we could not tell who was who.

Mother is happy because tonight we are sleeping still and quietly, not attracting unwanted attention. As long as others do not discover our whereabouts, mom will keep us here. She prepares us with the idea that we may have to move to another location upon detection. When she takes her trips to the dumpster, mom has also been scouting out a safe, alternate location for us. It is nice to not have to be concerned about any of this since mom seems well prepared. Having always lived on her own outside she has learned just what to do to survive. Now that she has us to look out for, keeping us safe has become her main priority.

The night quickly passes. Awakening with a ravenous hunger, we fortunately do not have to go far for a meal. Mom is ready with her sweet, warm milk. Since there are only four of us, we do not have to compete for a good place to eat. Once my belly is full I notice the daylight beginning to stream through the opening. I gaze at my beautiful mother getting ready to go out briefly to her dumpster. She warns us all once again to stay quiet and patiently await her return. "I'll be back as quickly as I can," she says.

My sisters are not listening. They are consumed with watching little brother beginning to open his eyes for the first time. We are all excited for him knowing the wonder that will fill his day. Their mews encourage him as well as occupy us while mom is gone. It's amusing to watch him as he struggles with the brightness, recalling that this was me only yesterday.

"I can see," he shouts, "The colors are even better than you described, orange tabby!"

"Look at us, little brother," the girls call to him.

He looks at them with a big smile, and then asks, "When will mother be back? I can't wait to see her. I know she will be beautiful!" We assure him that she is the most beautiful mother anyone could ever have.

Before long she returns. Little brother runs to her to get a good look. "You're beautiful! The others were right," he says to her.

"Thank you, I think you are too," she says as she licks little brother's head letting him know how proud she is of him. Since she has begun grooming with him, mother decides that this will be a good time for all of us to have a little grooming. Obediently, I await my turn, secretly anticipating the complete attention that I will receive from mom. Finally, she comes to me, beginning with my head. Her rough tongue is just wet enough to clean my face and ears. I close my eyes and envelop myself with her complete devotion, confident that she is expressing the deepest form of love for me.

Following all the activity of the early morning, my siblings and I soon tire. Mom, satisfied with all that she has accomplished, is beginning to feel a bit weary too. One by one, we soon settle in for a carefree midmorning rest. We stretch out for a silent siesta, lulled by the howls of the winds outside. Although our shelter is crude, we are well shielded from the harsh weather that looms on the other side of the opening. I hope that it will not be long before we have grown enough for mother to allow us to venture beyond our present limits. For today, however, it's enough just to imagine what awaits us on the other side.

Sensing our inquisitiveness, mother reveals to us her experiences with the outside in bits and pieces. Telling us enough each time to satisfy our curiosity, she always leaves us wanting more. Mother first describes to us the grass that we will feel under our paws when we first leave our home. It's a greenish color, darker than her eyes. In the morning the grass is covered with a layer of wetness which is cold and startling at first. Somehow, as the morning passes, the grass becomes drier and more pleasant to walk on. Mother is not sure how this happens; she only knows she much prefers to walk on this drier grass. "Some days, the water falls from the sky and the grass stays wet all day," she says. These are the days that she likes to take shelter and enjoy a long rest in solitude.

Other days, when the grass dries, there is warmth that can be felt from the bright light. There is nothing more enjoyable than basking in this light in the afternoon. Feeling her fur absorb the heat, her whole body fills with soothing warmth. It has been quite a while since she has been privileged to feel this luxurious sensation. With the distant look in her eyes as she tells us about it, it is evident that these are the moments that are the most wonderful for a cat living outside.

Her daily excursions to the mysterious dumpster also call for a detailed description. When leaving our home, mom cautiously looks and listens trying to detect the presence of anyone that could cause her harm. "Always be aware of what's around you," she warns.

Believing she is in the clear, she quickly makes her way under a row of unkempt hedges. The thick shrubs provide her with ample covering to avoid her from being spotted. At the end of the hedges is a hole in an old, dilapidated wooden fence. Her petite body fits through with ease depositing her into the large parking lot of the restaurant.

Again she must survey the circumstances that surround her, cautious of any danger that may be present. There is generally not a lot of activity occurring in this area early in the morning, which is why she chooses this time to search out a meal. Feeling relatively safe, mother gracefully leaps to the lip of the rusty dumpster. Balancing as only a cat can, she proceeds with her mission. Scraps of leftover food from the night before are a welcoming sight. Usually she only needs to dig a little to uncover some half eaten meatballs or a piece of tender chicken. Hastily, she devours her findings until her hunger is satisfied.

Licking her lips, she leaps back out of the dumpster onto the concrete surrounding. Glancing around, she scampers back to the hole in the fence. Once through, she navigates her way back through her trail under the brush. Eager to reunite with her kittens, she runs through the cold, wet grass to the opening under the shed. Squeezing through, mother is relieved to see her babies safely awaiting her return.

My sister, the calico, is never content with the stories mom tells us. Always feeling a need to ask her many questions, sis wants to know why mom is always worried about impending dangers. What is the threat that constantly compels her to be so carefully hidden? "Why is it so important to be so cautious all of the time?" asks calico.

Our ever patient, loving mother attempts to clarify her fearfulness as gently as she can. "The outside is vast, filled with lots of danger," she says. "There are large, fierce animals lurking about that are readily prepared to fight should you meet them."

Unfortunately mom witnessed the accidental disturbance of a raccoon by one of her fellow felines. Knife-like claws combined with razor-sharp teeth, an angry, challenged raccoon need only strike briefly to cause deep gashes and wounds to its victim. Recovering from such an attack is a long, painful process making the injured cat vulnerable to other predators.

The raccoon is only one of many animals to avoid. There are opossums, skunks, groundhogs and, occasionally, an unfriendly cat on the prowl for new territory to claim. Calico brags, "I could outrun any of those animals! I'm not afraid of them in the least."

Scolding her for foolishly discounting her warnings, mother is concerned that the scrappy personality of this kitten will surely lead her into trouble. "Pay attention!" she shouts, "What I'm telling you is important. This isn't a joking matter; you should take my stories seriously."

The rest of us listen intently, heeding the advice and gratefully accepting the wisdom passed on to us. Little brother cringes at the thoughts of what he has learned and the information compounds his skittishness. "I'm never going out there!" he insists. "Don't worry about that now," she reassures him. "When you're ready, you'll know."

My other sister and I absorb the information we receive choosing to worry about these situations only when we shall be faced with them. As long as we are under the watchful eye of our caring mother we only need think of the moment at hand, just as we are enjoying resting now.

As we lie sleeping in an intertwined huddle, an unfamiliar thumping noise abruptly awakens us. Instantly alert, mother raises her head and puts back her ears. The strange sound appears to originate from above. Little brother lets out a frightened squeal as every hair rises on his back. He is swiftly silenced by mom who tells us all to hush and remain still. "Shhh!! Don't move or make a sound!" exclaims mom.

Accompanying the thumping sound is that of muffled voices. We sit motionless, focused on the new and unusual noises. Once again, my uncontrollable imagination whisks me away to a place of sensational fantasy. The pounding becomes louder, concentrated directly above us. I fear the worst. Will the rotting wood above keep out this menacing being?

Retreating to the furthest corner we can find, my siblings and I struggle to hide from view. Mother does not follow. Instead, her protective instincts automatically give her the courage to fight off the mangy monster.

Bang! Bang! Bang! The methodical pounding will undoubtedly weaken the disintegrating wooden floor that is our ceiling. Splintering, the wood starts to show signs of collapse, allowing the creature to be able to break through.

Inevitably, like the final blow to a birthday piñata, a fist bursts through the floor. Gasping, our fear is realized. Mother is clearly within reach of the enormous, hairy claw.

She hisses as she swats frantically, keeping the beast at bay. "Run!" she shouts to us.

"No! We won't leave you, mother!" we yell back.

"Go!" she orders. "I'll join you later!"

Surely we are all to die if we remain. With no other options, we reluctantly obey mother. My sisters and little brother escape through the opening first. Looking back before I exit, I watch mother, fending for her life.

The bleeding gashes she has inflicted upon the hideous creature do not even appear to phase it in the least. Persistent, it continues to try to grab hold of her.

"Come on, mother!" I plead with her in desperation.

Turning to run, the creature grasps onto her hind leg firmly. Mother yelps, squirming to get loose, while the fiend drags her little by little towards the hole in the floor.

"Go! Run, orange tabby!" she commands, still more concerned with my safety than her own.

I cannot leave her. Defiantly, I charge back to her rescue. Thinking quickly, I sink my teeth deep into the claw that clutches my mother's leg. The startling strike ultimately causes the beast to loosen its grip, providing mother with a brief chance for escape.

Together, we dash through the opening, successfully making it to the safe haven of the outdoors. Before the beast has recognized his defeat, we are in safe hiding with the others. My brave rescue makes me a hero to my family.

They praise my courageousness when, suddenly, out of the blue it occurs to me that I'm deep in a daydream, again. I shut my eyes tightly, releasing them very slowly, one eye at a time. Remembering the unpleasant reality of the situation I had unconsciously drifted away from, I look around to see if anyone has become aware of my unintentional absence of mind.

Fortunately, the intensity of the situation has kept them from noticing. I remain still, wondering what will happen next. Who is making that curious thud? Could it be as terrible as I had imagined?

After what seems like an eternity, the sounds disappear leaving an eerie, lingering stillness. Each of us keeps our gaze fixed upon mother as we wait for further direction. She allows more time to pass before addressing our bewildered expressions.

Easing her posture to a more relaxed position, she signals to us that the danger has passed. We follow her lead and release the tension we have held within our little bodies. Mother knows just what had happened. It was caused by one of the most mystifying creatures she has encountered. She begins her explanation by calling them "people".

When she was younger she remembers an older woman who would kindly leave a bowl of food near the back door for her. Although mom would never venture close enough to the woman to be touched, she felt that the old woman meant her no harm. "Poor little kitty," the old woman would say, "Are you hungry? How about a nice bowl of food?

Come on, it's okay!" The woman seemed to understand and sympathize with my mother's hesitation to befriend her. Even though she did not appear to pose any threat to mom, experience had taught her to maintain a safe distance.

This relationship continued this way for a very long time. The old woman would put out food and mom would rush to eat when she was back in the house. It had become quite a comfortable and reliable routine until one day there was no old woman or bowl of food. For days, mom watched and waited for the woman to open the door and present her with a good meal. The growling from the hunger of her empty stomach forced her to seek out another food source. Traveling through numerous yards led her to a variety of people. Some would yell at her to scat, one cruel child threw a large stone and yet another chased her with a dog. None exhibited to her the kindness shown by the old woman.

Finally, exhausted and starving, she happened upon her restaurant dumpster. Glad to have a full stomach, mother learned how unpredictable a person's behavior can be. With other animals she usually knew what to expect, but some people, it seemed, were aggressive and others were gentle and comforting. A cat living outside has no means of knowing which a person will be, therefore must wisely choose not to trust any.

As for the noise from above, she knew from the voices that it meant people. Mother warned us, "Always be skeptical when in contact with a person even if they seem to be genuinely friendly. Never get too close," was her first instruction, and "Be ready to run for cover at all times," was her next.

Pondering whether or not it was still safe for us to remain in our current residence after this incident posed quite a dilemma for mom. Perhaps the people would not return and were not aware of our living under their shed. Moving us to a new location invited additional risks. The new home might not provide the same security as this one plus we could be seen making the trek. We were not yet as skilled as mom in the art of traveling swiftly and subtly. After much deliberation mom arrived at a conclusion. "We're going to remain where we are for now," she announced. "Hopefully, the people won't return, but if they do, the only thing for us then would be to move." Eventually we would outgrow this dwelling, forcing us to find a better suited living situation. Presently, however, it would be best to stay under our shed until we grew a little bigger.

The excitement of the day gradually drew to a close, leaving us all with an unprecedented feeling of fatigue. Reflecting on the day's events, we gathered into our usual sleeping arrangements. Little brother would be the first to snuggle close to mom, and then my sisters and I would join in. Calico was especially quiet this evening following the excitement of the day. Not her usual boastful self, somehow she had been humbled by the sudden fear she had so intensely felt. Our eyes were heavy, and as we lay down our heads, sleep came almost instantaneously.

The next morning, none of us were surprised when calico woke as her usual spirited self. The temporary effects of the previous day had completely worn off. "Good morning!" she said snickering; "Who's ready to play? I bet you can't catch me today, sis!"

With the start of a new day and a refreshing night's sleep, we were all feeling less bothered by the previous day's events. My gray sister initiated a friendly romp with little brother while my mother had gone for breakfast. She crouched down glaring at my unsuspecting little brother, wiggled her rear quarters, pouncing with less than precision. Tackling little brother onto his back they wrestled playfully. Enviously, calico and I rushed to join in the revelry. Each of us took turns pouncing and chasing one another resulting in an amicable skirmish.

Mother returned momentarily. She was pleased to watch us practicing our skills. My gray sister was an especially talented pouncer. Her timing was impeccable, always managing to catch me off guard, therefore giving her the advantage of the surprise of attack. She was definitely the fastest and most agile of our litter.

CHAPTER TWO

Dad

$\mathcal{A}$s the days flew by, the rate at which we grew stronger and larger was astounding. Mother had to be sure to eat plenty to keep up with our demand for her milk. Our days were filled with eating, playing, and sleeping. Mother continued to tell us stories, always trying to teach us a valuable lesson.

One gloomy, rainy day she chose to embark upon a portrayal of our father. Mother had not spoken of him often. Our knowledge of our father was limited to that of little brother's resemblance to him. Not knowing why she suddenly decided to divulge to us this information, we sat captivated, clinging to every word.

Her tale commenced with their first encounter. Mother had been rummaging through the dumpster, when she suddenly noticed another cat perched on the edge peering in at her. His expression was that of surprise and elation to discover her in this locale. He greeted her with soft mews and she returned the pleasantry.

"I live in the house across the street," he said, trying to impress her. "My owners mistakenly left the door open and

I made a break for it. What are you doing in this dumpster?" he asked.

Mother explained about the old woman and her search for food which led her to the dumpster. She then asked, "I've found some delicious chicken here, would you like to share it with me?"

Father declined, having eaten his fill before leaving his home. Mother shrugged, continuing to consume all that she could while she had the chance. Finishing her last bites, she asked, "What's it like living with a person?"

"I live with a whole family now. They adopted me last month, before that I lived with an old couple and a lot of other cats in a foster home," father replied. He continued to explain what it meant to be in a foster home noticing the inquisitive look on mother's face along with the perplexed tilt of her head. "My new family came one day and visited with all of the cats. They chose me, and named me Harley," he said. "The couple who took care of me told me that I was a lucky cat because Christmas was coming. That's when a lot of cats get adopted."

They sat together that whole afternoon exchanging tales about themselves. Mom told dad about her distrust for people warning him to be cautious. Father, coming from a different background, was amused by her street savvy. He had been lucky enough to have been with only gentle and kind people who took only the best care of him. He related to her his life with his new family. "There's always more than enough food for me," he said, "and they're constantly petting me and brushing my fur."

"If it's as wonderful as you say, then why did you run out the door?" asked mother.

"I was curious about what was out here," he said. "I thought it would be fun to explore a little."

As evening drew near, mother told him that it would be wise to seek shelter. She offered to let him stay with her in a safe place under a front porch that she often frequented. There was a strong attraction between them despite their obvious differences. Father was a well groomed, fun-loving house cat. Mother was more of a mangy, hardened street cat. Dad consented to go with her, he had not bargained for such an adventure when he had left his house.

Mother led the way as they reached the entrance to the porch. There was a hole in the lattice surrounding the porch, allowing just enough space for them to enter. Once inside, father looked around. The floor was composed of dirt with small rocks. It was dark and damp; he noticed how none of this bothered mother. She was content just to have a dry, safe place to sleep for the night. The dusky end to the day became illuminated with their discernible affection. Father ceased to be disturbed with his crude, short-term home, blinded by his infatuation with mother. She was also taken with the romantic companionship she had found in father. Having found her mate, she nuzzled against the soft fur of his chest falling into a deep, tranquil sleep.

During the night, father found it difficult to sleep. Dad was used to sleeping in a soft, warm bed. He whispered to mother, "Are you asleep?" She did not respond. He had not realized that the nights outside were much too cold for his indoor fur coat. Being an inside cat, he felt the winter weather keenly. Mother had grown a thick coat, insulating her from the freezing elements.

While she slept, father appreciated the precious time they had spent together, reluctantly admitting to himself the practicality of the situation. He was not equipped to be an outdoor cat. His fur would not keep him warm enough, plus he was accustomed to the luxuries of living with his family, whom he was beginning to miss. Throughout the night he anguished over how he would tell mom he had to return to his home and family. Perhaps, he contemplated, she would come back with him. His family would surely love her as much as he did. He knew the chances of this possibility were slim. She had established herself as an outdoor cat. She was as rooted in her lifestyle as he was in his, but he had to try.

At the break of dawn, mom began to stir. She opened her eyes to see dad looking lovingly back at her. "Good morning, you slept well," he said.

"I slept very well," she said. "It was nice to have the company. How did you sleep on your first night outside?"

"Honestly, not so well. My fur isn't as thick as yours and I must say that I'm starting to miss my home and family. I don't think that I'm meant to be an outside cat," he confessed.

"Do you think that you could get used to it?" she asked. She already knew the answer having considered this as a possibility previously. It's not an easy life, there's a lot to learn in order to survive from day to day.

"Actually, I was hoping that you might be able to get used to being an indoor cat. Please think about it before you say anything," he said. He was hoping that by some small miracle she would agree to this idea.

She looked away as she attempted to imagine herself in those circumstances. She could not, her place was the outdoors. It was what she knew, plus her fear of people was too great to overcome, even if it meant she could not be with him. "I'm sorry," she said with her head lowered. "I want to go with you to your home, but I know I wouldn't be happy there."

"I expected you'd say that," he said disappointedly. "Maybe we can agree to meet when the weather is warmer. I'll sneak out of my home and look for you."

She agreed to these terms as it seemed the only logical solution. There was a long silence when suddenly dad's ears perked up. He heard his name being called in the distance. "Harley, here kitty! Please come back Harley!" a child's voice was shouting.

He knew this voice. "I must go now," he said to mom. "I'll come back and find you." She nodded her head. He nuzzled her, turning and running to a little girl who scooped him up in her arms, holding him tightly.

"I knew we'd find you! I've missed you so much Harley, why did you run out?" she asked him.

Mom watched as they walked back in the direction of their house. That was the last time mom had seen him. She does not regret the time they shared that day. Even though they must live separately, they had developed a lasting bond.

Weeks had passed since mom's memorable day with dad. She had come to discover, however, that she was to have kittens. Her time and attention turned to preparation for this blessed event. Between her extra trips to the dumpster and scouting out an acceptable place to deliver her kittens she paused to reflect on father. The next time they should meet she would introduce him to their kittens.

After mom finished her story about dad, my sisters, brother and I were all thinking the same thing. We looked at one another wondering who would volunteer to ask. To our surprise we heard little brother question nervously, "When can we meet our dad?"

"Well, I have a surprise for you. I didn't expect to see him for a few weeks when the weather becomes warmer, but when I went for breakfast, there he was! He said he missed me terribly so he snuck out of his house for the day. Would you like to meet him now?" she said with a smile.

"Yes! Yes! Hurry!" we all shouted.

We could hardly contain our excitement. Meeting our dad for the first time was an extremely thrilling adventure for us. We understood now why it was that mother had chosen today to tell us the story of dad. Mom let out a meow to signal him that we were ready. Father pushed his head in slowly, wriggling his body through the opening, he slipped in.

"Well, what an incredibly good looking bunch! I'm so happy to see all of you," he said.

We raced to greet him. My gray sister was the first to climb onto his back as he lay on the dirt floor.

"This one looks like you," he said to mother.

"And this one looks like you," she said to father, pointing to my little brother. "Plus we have a gorgeous calico and an adorable orange tabby."

"What are their names?" he asked.

"I've never considered it. Usually outdoor cats do not have names," she answered.

"Well," he said smiling. "We must talk about this later."

She agreed, proud to finally share with him their beautiful kittens.

"Dad, are you going to stay with us here under the shed from now on?" asked the ever inquisitive calico.

"Nothing would make me happier," he told her. "But, I'm an indoor cat and can't stay. I do live close and will try to come often," he added. The thought of only seeing them on occasion saddened our dad. He wondered if mother would allow at least one of them to go home with him when they were big enough. He decided to approach this subject with her later when they were alone. For now, he would enjoy this time with his energetic, vivacious kittens.

We tumbled, climbed and played, making the most of every moment we had with father. "They're very active," he said to mother, thinking we would never grow tired.

"Full of energy," she muttered. Mom was resting in the corner, taking full advantage of the situation. It was nice not to have to keep a watch on us for a little while.

Eventually, we did exhaust ourselves. Fighting off the need for sleep as long as we could, sleep finally took over. Father took this opportunity to retreat back to his home. "It'll be easier if there are no sad goodbyes. When they wake, tell them I'll return when I can," he whispered to mom.

She decided to walk back part way with him. He was glad she had accompanied him, allowing them to talk. "It was a real surprise today to find out we have kittens! You've taken really good care of them, they're wonderful. I'm glad that I decided to come out today for a visit," he said.

"I'm happy too. I didn't think that I'd see you for a few weeks. The kittens were also very excited to meet their father. I didn't talk a lot about you until today in case you couldn't come when you wanted to," said mom.

Dad thought this would be a good time to discuss his bringing home some kittens with her. "I was thinking," he said with hesitation, not sure what her reaction would be. "Maybe when they're a bit bigger I could take at least one or two kittens home with me. It would make it easier for you to care for them, plus the kittens would have a good home."

He was pleasantly surprised when mother approved of this suggestion. "It's a lot of work to keep track of them. It would surely be easier to teach and care for fewer kittens. How many would you be able to take with you? It would be good for them all to have a home as good as yours," she said. Mother was relieved by his offer. She had been thinking of what she would do with these babies when they were older. If they could have a home like dad's, they would be well cared for. She would be free then to return to looking out only for herself.

"I'll start with two. Let me see how my family reacts. Find a fair way to choose which ones should come with me first. When I return to visit you I'll take them back with me," said dad.

"It won't be easy, but I'll do my best. They're getting big fast and I'll soon have to let them out from under the shed for a little exploring," said mom. "Also, we heard people in the shed once, if they return we'll have to move."

In agreement, they nuzzled not wanting to part. "I must get back to the kittens before they wake," said mother.

"I need to go too," said father, reluctantly. "I'll see you soon," he said, sauntering back to his home. His head was held high with pride thinking of his newly found family.

Father's offer left mom with a sense of encouragement. Having a safe and loving home for her kittens was a comforting thought. Now all that was left was to decide which two kittens should be the first to go. Without a doubt, she knew that my little brother was the first choice. His reluctance to venture beyond his immediate surroundings, accompanied by his timid, shy ways made him the foremost choice, even before the girls. She was sure she would send him first.

Selecting from the remaining three posed a dilemma. My gray sister was the fastest, calico was tenacious and I was a male. Since she was already sending one boy, mom thought that she would eliminate me as an option. Reflecting for a while, she realized the best solution was to discuss the situation with the girls, letting them arrive at a conclusion. Returning to her sleeping litter, confident with her plan of action, mom silently crept through the opening and tried to join them in their peaceful sleep.

CHAPTER THREE

Separation

"I want to go!" shouted my gray sister. "I thought dad was lots of fun."

"That's perfect!" calico added. "I want to stay with mother. I haven't had a chance to explore the outside yet. I'll stay with mom and orange tabby investigating everything we can."

"Yes!" I said to calico. "We'll have lots of fun together, once we leave the shed." I didn't wish to reveal to them the true reason for my being happy to stay. I was not yet prepared to separate from mom. Still feeling a need to be with her, I was more than content with the arrangements.

Of course little brother was elated to not have to experience the frightening outside world. He was meant to be a pampered house cat with no worries. Mom was also satisfied with our resolution. This decision had not been as difficult as she originally had thought.

"We don't have a lot of time left altogether. I'll miss you, gray kitten and little brother, but I know father will give you a good home. "I'm happy that you'll have wonderful lives!" mother said, with just a hint of sadness in her voice.

Knowing our remaining time together was limited, we relished every moment. Our days were filled with speculating about what was to come. We had not known anything but the world under our shed with mother. None of us would admit to our growing fears, not even little brother. Mother would never allow us to go anywhere that she did not deem safe. Trusting her instincts, we patiently waited for father's return.

"I wonder if father's family will keep us in their home?" gray sister said to little brother.

"I hope that we can stay together. Do you think they'll give us names?" he asked her.

She laughed as she answered, "Of course, all house cats have names, silly!"

"Silly! Maybe that will be your name, gray sister!" mocked calico with her usual sassiness. "While you're getting names, orange tabby and I will be on an adventure outdoors, until it's our turn to go with father."

"Do you think mother will let us go with her to the dumpster, calico?" I asked her. Although it was selfish, I was looking forward more to having extra attention from mom, once little brother and gray sister had left, than exploring with calico.

"I'll ask her. I hope father takes a long time coming back for us so we can go everywhere mom goes!" she replied.

Listening to our conversation, mom wondered if she would ever be able to control calico after she had tasted freedom. "Orange tabby, I'll need your help keeping an eye on calico when she's outside," she whispered to me privately.

"You can count on me, mom!" I answered. Mom needs me now, I thought. We would be a team. I almost could not wait for the others to go. This thought did make me sad though, as I knew how much I would miss them both!

Every day we woke wondering if this would be the day of father's return. The darkness of the nighttime seemed shorter. The chilling temperatures also became more tolerable. Perhaps this is what mother meant by the weather getting warmer. Surprisingly, mother was allowing us to go to the opening, stick out our heads and peer out.

What we saw was remarkable. There was grass everywhere, but not the vivid green we had expected. Mother said that the colors would change, becoming more vibrant as the warmth from the bright light became stronger. Tall trees which housed industrious, brown squirrels towered well above our shed. Most days the sky was a dull gray, but on occasion it transformed into a scintillating hue of blue. We were fixated on the incredible world just beyond our humble abode.

"Can I just step right outside," calico continually begged mom.

"Soon enough, calico. One step at a time. Have patience, little one," mom would answer.

"How much longer until dad comes?" little brother pestered mother constantly. It was apparent that we were all becoming increasingly anxious for his arrival. How quickly we were growing, becoming ready for the next stage.

Tired and frustrated one afternoon, mother finally gave into the relentless badgering from calico. "Go ahead. Step just outside the shed. If you see any people, run back as fast as you can," she warned. "Orange tabby, you go with her and see that she listens."

Compliantly I answered, "Yes mother. We'll stay right there."

Calico could not believe mother agreed to let her outside. She was a little annoyed with the prospect of my chaperoning her, but was not in a position to argue. "Come on orange tabby, let's go!" she demanded.

The winds carried so many different, interesting smells which did not reach us under the shed. Thankfully, they provided enough distraction for calico to keep her frozen in place with her nose in the air. This made my assignment of watching her very easy. At last, mother called us back in. "More fun tomorrow, kittens. That's enough for today," said mom.

With each passing moment we all grew more and more restless. Mom was allowing us short jaunts just outside the shed each day. She knew this would only temporarily pacify the curious calico. "I expect father will come any day now," she assured us.

Each morning we wondered if we had spent our last night together. A strange sound awoke us very early this one morning. "What's that sound? Is it a fierce animal?" little brother asked trembling.

"No, not at all," said mother. "That's a sure sign that spring is near. It's the sound of a bird. The birds fly away in the cold weather, returning when it's warmer to have their babies. They're the ones that are afraid of us!"

We had a long laugh at the expense of poor little brother. He was not bothered by our snickering, only relieved with mom's answer. Our chuckling had been loud enough to prevent us from hearing the presence of approaching footsteps. Suddenly, without warning, we heard the tender voice of dad.

"What's all the ruckus in here?" he said, announcing his arrival.

"Dad, you've finally come!" clamored gray sister as she charged at him. "I'm ready to go!"

"Hold on there, not so fast. I want to spend a little time visiting with everyone first," he told her.

Mother interrupted, "You'll be taking little brother and gray sister first. When you come back the next time orange tabby and calico will go with you."

"We really have to get them names," he reminded her. "I've chosen today to come because I heard my owners saying they'd like to get another cat soon to keep me company. Can you imagine the luck? I thought the kittens would just about be ready to leave you now too."

"Does that mean we'll live with you in your house, dad?" little brother said hopefully.

"There's a strong possibility. My human family is very loving and caring, I know they will fall in love with the two of you," he said.

Mom thought how nice it would be to be able see them every once in a while. Everything seemed to be falling into place perfectly for our family. Father stayed a long time with us that day. We were very fortunate kittens to have such adoring parents.

Morning quickly turned into afternoon. With heavy eyes, mother and father began yawning, indicating their desire for a long afternoon nap. Ordinarily, father would curl up on a fuzzy, blue blanket in the darkness of a bedroom closet. His family respected his quite predictable routine, always remembering to leave the door cracked open to allow him to enter. Before the drowsiness intensified, he stood up stretching first his front legs then his rear.

Mom recognized his cue and said to him, "I suppose it's time for you to go now."

"Yes," he answered her. "Are you ready little brother and gray sister? Say good bye now," he said.

This was the moment we had waited for, but none of us had anticipated exactly how hard saying good bye would be. Bravely, mom said, "Don't worry little kittens; you'll be well cared for. Your father's family is good and will see to it that you're taken care of. I'll miss you. Always remember how much I love you."

She took a moment to nuzzle them both, licking their heads. Mom wanted them looking their best to meet their new families.

Calico joined their huddle, flashing a look at me saying I should follow. Deciding to lighten the situation, I crouched down into a pounce position directed right at gray sister.

Before she knew what had happened, I leaped on her knocking her over. "Gotcha!" I gloated.

Laughter instantaneously replaced the tears we were holding back. "When we meet again I want a rematch!" gray sister said to me.

Seeing his opportunity to leave us with smiles, father said, "Good bye, I'll be back for the others when the time is right. Follow me little ones."

Father turned, walking away slowly at first. Calico and I watched as little brother and gray sister raced to keep up with father's long strides. Mother sat quietly, knowing she had done her best for them. Turning the corner, they disappeared from our sight. Mother jumped to her feet. "Stay here, I want to watch them go into their new house. I'll be right back," she said.

Mother quickly trotted undetected behind them. She hid in the bushes across the street from father's house. Reaching his front door with his two little kittens, he scratched and meowed until it was opened. The girl who had come for him before looked out at them in disbelief. "Mother! Come quick! You'll never believe what Harley has brought home!" she screamed into the house.

An attractive, young woman came running. "Oh my, look at these babies! The one looks just like Harley. These must be his kittens. I wonder where they've been all this time," she exclaimed. Looking at dad she said in a matter of fact voice, "Harley, it's time to have you fixed. I'm afraid we've neglected this."

They picked up little brother and gray sister, who purred on cue. "They're adorable! Can we keep them mom?" begged the little girl. "I'll name the gray one, Smokey and the boy, Oliver!"

"Well, I suppose they do need a home. We were thinking about another cat anyway. We'll see, it may just work out. Let's take them inside and talk to Dad," her mom answered.

Mom watched as they entered the home. They have names, she thought, they'll be okay. With a sigh of relief she paused for only a second to dwell on this moment. Remembering calico and me anxiously waiting for her to come back, she ran all the way as fast as she could to us.

Telling us every detail of what she'd witnessed, we were thrilled for "Oliver" and "Smokey". "Let's take a rest now, it's been a long day," said mom.

The absence of our siblings left an unsettling void which we knew would take some time to get used to. As I closed my eyes to fall into sleep, I thought how empty it would be here for mom once calico and I had also departed. Sympathetically, I curled up with her, reassuring her that she would always be loved.

CHAPTER FOUR

Exploration

Wasting no time in accomplishing her mission to accompany mom everywhere, calico impertinently asked, "When will we be going to the dumpster for dinner?"

Recognizing that calico was not yet prepared to make this journey, mom replied delicately, "Calico, I know that you really want to come with me, but I think we need to make sure orange tabby is also ready for the trip." She winked at me as she asked, "Orange tabby, how do you feel about going to the dumpster so soon? Wouldn't you like to spend a few more days practicing for danger first?"

Knowing the answer mom was expecting, I immediately responded, "Oh yes, let's practice a little more first, calico, there will be plenty of time to go with mom."

Mom's cunning plan worked, calico conceded reluctantly, aware that she was outnumbered. "Why don't you play for a bit outside?" mom added.

Mom's suggestion that we play right outside the opening for a while furnished an opportunity for calico and I to prove our worthiness to mother. "Okay, orange tabby, let's see who can run the fastest," she challenged.

We walked together, away from the opening, turning around at a pre-established distance. On the count of three we dashed back as rapidly as our little legs would carry us. Our races were always very close. Each time, however, calico would venture a tad bit farther from the shed. She derived great pleasure from mischievously pushing the limits mother had set for her.

Completely preoccupied with our games, calico and I hadn't paused to consider our missing siblings. In fact, we deliberately attempted to avoid acknowledging the empty space that remained. To dwell upon their absence would not be constructive, especially for mother.

Calico and I rumbled and tumbled for hours training for the possibility of an encounter with an unfriendly sort. Practicing mock fights, our matches, at times, would escalate too quickly, requiring interference from mother. "That's enough kittens! Somebody's going to get hurt," she'd yell.

When night fell, mother, calico and I snuggled closely. Without control, during the quiet stillness, my mind speculated about Oliver and Smokey's new life. I pictured them, warm and cozy, sleeping on a feathery soft bed. Soon calico and I would join them, enjoying the comforts of a home. Peacefully, I closed my eyes. It didn't take long to fall into a deep sleep following our extremely active days.

The next few days proved uneventful. The unseasonably mild weather permitted us ample time for play. We began to sense that the temporary reprieve we were experiencing was coming to a sudden close. Cool winds ushered in, causing us to shudder. The clear blue skies developed dark gray, ominous clouds. "It won't be long before the water starts to fall from the sky and we must take cover," mother warned us.

"When it stops can we go back out?" calico asked.

"As long as it hasn't gotten dark or too cold," promised mom. "Before the water falls, I'm going to go get dinner. You're both to wait under the shed for my return. I'll try not to be too long."

Hastily, mother whisked us into the opening under the shed. "Be good, I'll be right back," she said.

Mother had not been gone for but a moment when calico turned to me with a devilish grin and said, "Let's go out for one more romp before mother gets back."

"But, she told us to wait here, calico. I don't know," I rebuffed.

"Don't be a baby, she won't even know. We're ready to go with her, but she still thinks we aren't! At least we can have some fun while she's gone," said calico, halfway out of the opening.

"Wait!" I shouted. "Mom's going to be cross with us!"

She didn't listen; there was no changing her mind. What should I do? Mother told us to stay and wait, but she also told me to keep an eye on calico. I feared I would be in trouble either way. I had to follow calico, perhaps I could persuade her to come back before mom ever knew we left.

"Just one race, calico, and then back under the shed... okay?" I implored her.

"We'll see who wins first," she taunted.

That calico! She was going out farther than we'd ever gone before. Surely mother would catch us outside and we'd both be in big trouble. Running to catch up to her, I kept shouting, "Please stop, calico!"

Ignoring my pleas she continued, until finally she stopped, panting and laughing. Rumbles of thunder escorted with dark, foreboding storm clouds approached swiftly. All I could hear when we paused to catch our breath was the loud thumping of my little, racing heart.

"Look how far we are, orange tabby," said calico. "This will be our best race yet!"

Recovering from the long, strenuous chase, I raised my head with trepidation. "Calico, what have you done?" I snapped at her. "We'll never beat mother back now!"

Just then, in the distance, I caught a glimpse of mother nearing the shed. "Look, there's mother. What are we going to do now?" I asked her.

It was too late! Mother spotted us, far from our shed. It was hard to hear her as she screeched at us. What was she trying to say? She looked panicked, not angry as I expected. "Quiet, calico. What's mom saying?" I said, hushing her.

"She's yelling 'Look out!'" said calico puzzled.

"Look out for what?" I questioned.

With all the commotion, we had not noticed the presence of danger that crept upon us. Without warning, calico and I were snatched from the ground by the scuff of our necks. Frantically we hissed and swatted with our tiny, sharp claws unable to reach anything.

Suspended in the air, what happened in a few seconds seemed to last an eternity. I could hear mother howling helplessly in the background as our captor flung us carelessly into some sort of sac. The water from the sky had begun to drizzle upon us. I glanced for an instant at the face of our assailant. It was worse than I had imagined, it was a person.

He was an older man with a straggly brown beard. Rimmed glasses covered what remained of his pasty, pale face. Although he was not large for a person, his size was quite intimidating to us. He sneered down at us as we huddled together trapped in the bag. Opening his mouth to reveal his crooked, yellowed teeth he boasted; "Now I've got ya! Live under my shed, will ya!"

There was something familiar about that voice. Instantly it came to me. That was one of the voices we heard above us in the shed that day. I was sure of it. What would he do with us? Mother was right to be leery of him. Oh no, poor mother! What would she tell father when he came for us? How heartbroken she would be without us. An overwhelming feeling of guilt added to my state of panic.

Calico was bawling uncontrollably. Comforting her was what I must set my mind to. It would be what mother wanted. "Stay close to me, calico, we'll be all right," I reassured her, even though I feared the worst.

What could make this human treat us so cruelly? Did our cries have no affect whatsoever on his hard heart? This man must have had a mother of his own at one time. How could he take us away from ours this way?

Unbelievably, the fact that we were in the midst of a serious crisis did not prevent my mind from wondering elsewhere. Drifting away, I pictured this tyrannical person as a little child. Next to his mother, he was so small and helpless, almost appealing. She was not the nurturing, loving kind of mother that I was used to. There was a callous, arrogant sense about her. The child was crying, reaching out for the comfort of his mother's arms. Pushing him away, it was obvious that she merely tolerated his existence, but did not care for him.

Consumed only with herself, she completely neglected him.

"Shut up, you brat!" she finally squawked at him.

Wailing louder, he struggled to catch his breath. Those cries in my daydream seemed so very real. Wait! Those sobs are real! They are coming from calico. Forcing my mind to return, I focused on consoling poor, frightened calico.

The horrible man never must have learned how to care or feel affection. All he ever knew was disregard and unkindness. I could almost feel sorry for him, if I weren't so terribly worried about what he was going to do to us.

What would our fate be? I predicted the most dreadful outcomes. We could be lobbed into a frozen river, sure to drown. He could leave us in the middle of the woods, without food and be prey to the larger animals. Numerous scenarios ran through my mind. I mustn't mention any of this to calico, it would only cause her more alarm.

"I want mother! I'm sorry for going so far. I'm so scared, orange tabby!" she quivered.

The man had closed the bag. Surrounded by darkness we could hear the water falling heavily from the sky, tapping the outside of the bag. Transporting us with a hastened pace, the man moved us further and further away from the sounds of mother's cries. Abruptly we were halted with a hard thump. No longer were we in motion, but trapped within the bag tossed onto something. Another loud thump preceded the first, followed by the sound of a car engine. There was no longer the sound of the water falling or mother. We must not be outside anymore, I thought.

"Where are we now?" calico managed to ask.

"I don't know, calico. That man must be taking us somewhere," I answered.

"How will we ever get back to mother?" she wondered. I could not answer her. We were not going back, that was the reality. Calico was not ready to hear this news. Instead of talking about it, I huddled with her as closely as I could.

The movement of the vehicle gave us an uneasy sensation. Being frightened more than ever, instinctively we incessantly screamed for help. Our petrified weeping must have agitated the hardhearted man, resulting with him vehemently shouting, "Shut up you stupid cats! You are more trouble than you are worth!"

At last, after a long ride, the car screeched to a halt. The clanking sound of the engine persisted even though we were no longer moving. Dreading what was coming next, calico and I clung to one another desperately. Listening intently for any clue as to our whereabouts, we heard the car door creak open. Our bag was forcibly lifted from where it had settled. "Hold on tightly!" I ordered calico.

"Good riddance!" the man muttered.

Whirling through the air, we landed with a hard thud. "Are you okay, orange tabby?" calico asked.

"I think so, are you?" I responded.

"Yes. Where do you think we are now?" she asked.

"I'm not sure," I said. Just then we heard the sound of a car racing away. "He must have thrown us into something. We need to try to get free."

The water plummeted from the sky, pelting the exterior of our bag. We could feel the wetness slowly seeping through onto our backs. The dampness created a chill, calico was shivering.

"I'm cold and getting hungry," she complained.

"Me too, calico. We have to try to get out of here," I told her. Searching in the darkness for an opening from which to escape was becoming hopeless. We could not get out. What were we to do? Would we ever manage to find mother again? Was she trying to find us? The disturbing thoughts lingered in my mind while I attempted to be brave for calico. We were getting wetter and colder. Would we ever be able to get out?

"Do you think the man will come back?" calico asked.

"I don't know. I hope not!" I answered.

At this point mother's fear of people became clear to me. Experiencing for myself how bad people could be, I empathized with her misgivings. Father's circumstances, on the other hand, showed how they could be genuinely kindhearted. Mother had obviously recognized the good, despite her misfortune, or Smokey and Oliver would not have homes now.

I was torn as to whether or not I could trust any person, ever. Both mother and father were right about people. Some were good and some were not. Learning how to tell the nice from the unkind was surely a special skill that only comes with time and experience. The mean man was obviously wicked, but I suspected we'd come across others who might not be what they seem.

CHAPTER FIVE

Discovery

$\mathcal{A}$ shuffling noise was coming from outside the bag. We stood very still with our ears perked up to listen. "Do you hear that?" I asked calico.

"Yes, what could it be? Is it the mean man? Maybe a ferocious animal? I'm scared!" she proclaimed.

Whatever it was, it grabbed our bag, hoisting us into the air. We heard a voice yell, "I've got it! I found what he threw into the dumpster!"

This was not the deep, raspy voice of the man. This voice was higher, like that of a young girl. "I knew it was suspicious when he drove up and quickly threw that bag into the dumpster in the middle of this torrential rain!" she said.

A male voice answered, "You were right. In this heavy rain, he didn't even see us looking out the back door. It's a good thing we happened to be there. Now, what's in the bag?"

She untied the bag, looking at us with disbelief she said, "You'll never guess. There are two adorable little kittens! What a horrible man!"

Remembering that it was difficult to know whether or not a person would be kind, we sat frozen, not sure how to react. Carefully dumping us out of the bag, they placed us in a large box with a soft, dry towel on the bottom.

"Careful not to get scratched," cautioned the girl. "They're scared and probably think we're going to hurt them."

We hissed our fiercest, warning them of our defensive, distrustful dispositions. After what we'd just been through, our fear of human beings was immense. Keeping up our guard, we vowed to put up a fight, if need be.

Trapped in the box, they just watched us from above. The girl was young, with medium length dark hair, which notably contrasted her very pale skin. Decorated fancily with oodles of flashy jewelry, she emitted a very potent, unfamiliar scent. The boy, on the other hand, was dressed in all black. His aroma was also very strong, but his jewelry was limited to one sparkling, gold earring.

Wisely, they didn't bother us at all. They just let us be. Before long we were warm and dry again. As the time passed, our fear of these people lessened. "I don't think they'll hurt us. What do you think, calico?" I whispered to her.

Nodding, she agreed, "I think we'll be all right, for now."

Feeling better, calico asked, "Did you hear her say we were in a dumpster? Maybe it was mother's dumpster and she's waiting for us outside?"

"I thought about that too. I didn't smell food and I think we are too far from home for it to be the same dumpster," I said. It was time to tell her, "Calico, I don't think that we'll ever be able to find our way back to mother, but I do think these people are nice and will help us."

Sobbing, she nuzzled against my chest, "I know you're right, I'm glad that you're with me orange tabby," she whimpered.

The two people were hovering over us, debating what they would do next. "Well," said the girl, "I'll bet they're hungry! Can you watch the shop while I walk over to the store next door to find them some food?"

"Sure, it isn't busy with this storm anyhow," he answered.

We were getting hungry; mother would have fed us by now. Thinking of mother made me ache. How would she feel alone without us tonight, not knowing what has happened to us? Surely she would not return to the shed with the threat of the man there. Maybe she would revert to her porch where she had brought father that night.

Thoughts of our predicament were becoming overrun with the growling pangs of hunger percolating in our empty stomachs. We had never known hunger like this before. Mother was always available with her milk. I was beginning to realize that nothing was going to be as it had been before.

Before long the girl reappeared. She placed a bowl with food along side of a bowl with water. We had never eaten food this way before. Carefully approaching the bowl, calico nudged me slightly saying, "Go ahead, you try it first."

"No problem," I said. "I'm starving and I'll try anything." I was pleasantly surprised with a savory feast. Plunging into the bowl, I continued to eat fervently.

Observing my indulgence, calico said, "Hey orange tabby, leave some for me!" Enthusiastically, she joined me. Together we devoured every last morsel, licking the plate clean! Once our appetites had been satisfied, we quenched our thirst with some fresh, cold water. "That was delicious!" said calico, washing her face with her paw.

"Wow! They were hungry!" exclaimed the girl.

"What are we going to do with them now? It's Sunday night, where could we bring them? No one will be open now," the boy said.

She stood quietly, thinking for a moment before she answered, "Well, we'll have to wait to call the shelter in the morning. They've been fed and will be warm and dry in the box until then. They will have to spend the night here in the store. I'll come in early tomorrow morning to take care of them."

"Okay, I suppose that would work. What if they're able to get out from the box?" he asked.

"Well, how about if we put the box into the bathroom, leave a little light on and close the door. That way if they do get out, they won't get far," she answered.

"That works for me, it's a good plan," he said.

They carried our box into the bathroom, turning on a small light. Calico and I were not afraid, these people seemed nice. Our bellies were stuffed, we were warm and safe and our eyes were becoming very heavy.

The girl looked down into our box and whispered, "You go to sleep and be good. I'll be back first thing in the morning to feed you and find a place to take you. Good night, little kittens."

The door closed behind her, leaving us all alone. Calico and I found ourselves exhausted from the day's events. Without saying a word, we knew just what the other was thinking... sleep. Retreating to the corner of the box, we rested our heads on one another, falling into a deep relaxing sleep the moment our eyes shut.

Endless hours seemed to pass, as we slumbered motionless together. Slowly dreams crept in, pleasant at first. I dreamt of Smokey, Oliver and calico playing with me under our shed. Images of mother, caring for and loving us also pervaded. Memories of the time spent with father, laughing and climbing brought a comfortable warm feeling to me.

Wanting this blissful state of tranquility to continue indefinitely, I resisted emerging from my dreams to a lighter stage of sleep. Unsuccessfully, however, disagreeable pictures of our present reality began to flash before me. I could see the face of the mean man, hear calico's frightened cries and remember the howls of our heartbroken mother. Being reminded of our current predicament and what led us to it made me fully awake.

Opening my eyes drowsily, I noticed calico stretching her legs, shifting her position. The long sleep had offered a necessary reprieve from our uncertain circumstances.

Rejuvenated, we were prepared to face a new day filled with discovery. Softly I asked, "Calico, are you awake?"

Yawning, she replied, "Yes. We really slept for a long time. Orange tabby, I want to go home so badly. I miss mother and the others so much!"

"Me too!" I said. "I keep thinking about how sad mother must be wondering where we are. I miss her a lot too."

"What do you think will happen to us today? That girl will come back. Where will she bring us?" calico asked.

"I don't know, calico. We can only hope it's somewhere nice," I said.

Calico began looking around the box, then up the sides. I could almost predict what she was going to say next. "Let's climb out and see what's out there," she blurted out.

Well, what did we have to lose? "Sure, why not?" I replied.

Calico attempted to scale the walls only to fall back to the bottom of the box. There was nothing to cling to for support. Then we had an idea. Stepping off of the edge of the food bowl would give us a boost. Standing on the side of the bowl, it flipped into the air landing against the side of the box. This was even better, we ascended the sides easily. At the top, we leaped off landing feet first onto the hard floor.

Immediately a victorious run ensued. Slipping and sliding on the sleek floor we chased each other all around the tiny room. "I'm having so much fun!" said calico, panting.

"I know! This is great!" I said. We were completely amused trying to run with a lack of traction ending up sprawled out on the floor.

A long strip of white toilet paper floating over us came to our attention during our wrestling match. "Look at that, calico," I said. "Catch it!"

Swatting at the paper, she managed to hook her front claw onto it. Running and tugging, the paper dispersed easily from its roll. Little effort was required to unravel the entire roll from the cardboard tubing. Surrounded in a cloud of white fluffy toilet paper we continued with our grappling.

This interesting place offered so much to explore. Preoccupied with curiosity, we didn't notice how quickly the time was passing or the rumbling beginning in our bellies. Calico and I were thoroughly enjoying sharing this unsupervised playtime.

Just then, the door swung open, giving us a startle. "What have you been doing?" the girl said shaking her head and laughing. "Well, I told you I'd be back. It's a good thing I borrowed a carrier from my neighbor! I can see you like to get into trouble. What a mess you've made."

"Don't let her catch you, calico. We don't want to be locked up…. Run," I shouted at her. We scurried away each time the girl attempted to catch us. This was a great game; it was what we had trained for when we ran our races.

"Well, this isn't working. I have an idea," the girl said. Opening the carrier cage, she placed a fresh bowl of food at the far end. "Now, let's see what happens."

Patiently sitting on the floor, she was no longer trying to catch us. After a while, we stopped running. "Why did she stop chasing us, orange tabby?" calico asked confused.

"I don't know, maybe she gave up and isn't trying to catch us anymore," I answered.

"She has put our food in that other box, should we go eat? I'm really getting hungry," calico said.

"I suppose, I'm starving!" I said.

Sitting very still, the girl only watched us. Entering the new box we thought of nothing but another delicious meal. Focusing on our eating, we did not notice the girl slowly moving towards the box. Suddenly, after hearing a click, we realized we were captured inside. There were plenty of holes in this box plus an opening at the end with bars allowing us to see out.

"Sorry," she said. "I had to catch you somehow."

Bringing the carrier into the store, she placed us onto the counter. Following a short phone conversation, she transported us outside to her car. Where were we going? Calico and I became frightened and began to cry.

"Don't worry. It's okay. I've found a shelter with a volunteer that will take you and find you both good homes. I promise you'll be safe and well cared for," the girl said, consoling us the best that she could.

Chapter Six

Rescue

"Hi," the girl said to the person sitting at the front desk. "I found these two little kittens yesterday. When I called this morning, I was told a volunteer here would be able to take them for foster care."

"Yes. I spoke to you. Judy will be taking them. She'll be here soon. You can leave them with me and I'll give them to her," replied the person.

Transferred to a larger cage, we could view our temporary surroundings better. Petting our heads through the bars, the girl said her good byes. Dogs were continuously barking in the background. A multitude of various scents wafted through our cage. "I wish we could escape to explore," said calico.

Not sharing in her curiosity, I longed for the shed and mother. "Calico, I just want to feel at home again like we did with mother. I'm glad you're with me, but I miss mother so much," I said sadly.

Staying close, we sat together in a cozy box filled with a cushion of clean litter. It was so much bigger and brighter here than we were used to. There was activity everywhere we looked. A myriad of cages were filled with dogs and cats of all types. A young girl with a big dog caught my eye. Her long brown hair was tied up in a pony tail with wispy bangs covering her forehead. Her old jeans were torn at the knee and topped with a light blue t-shirt. She was busy brushing a large black and brown dog with very matted fur.

"Poor girl! Don't worry; we'll get you looking beautiful again. My name is Jennie. What should we call you? How about Daisy?" she said to the dog, reassuringly.

Looking back at her with grateful, big brown eyes, the dog whimpered. It was as if the girl understood just what she was saying. "Don't fret about those puppies. The vet is checking them all out and you'll have them back soon enough."

Another girl walked in, she smiled at us then went over to lend a hand with Daisy. She was wearing a t-shirt identical to the one Jennie had on. She was much shorter and slimmer than Jennie with her dirty blonde hair in a short, styled hair cut.

"What's her story?" she asked Jennie.

"Hi, Sarah. It's so sad." Jennie began. "Someone found her tied to a tree in a park. In a box next to her were six tiny puppies! It's lucky they were found before the puppies got too cold."

"How could someone do something like that?" Sarah said, outraged.

"Whoever owned her probably didn't want to deal with her once she had the puppies and just chose to abandon her. From the condition she's in, they didn't take very good care of her either. She's filthy and underweight. I just hope the puppies make it," said Jennie.

"That really breaks my heart," said Sarah, stroking Daisy's head gently. "Where did those two kittens come from?" she asked, looking over at us.

Jennie shook her head and answered, "Those two were found in a bag in a dumpster during a rainstorm. They were just brought in. Judy said that she'd take them."

"I can't stand it! How can people treat them like that?" pondered Sarah.

"I've been volunteering here for years and you see it over and over. You never really get used to it. You just have to do the best for them once they're here," said Jennie.

"I suppose. This is going to be a harder job than I thought," grumbled Sarah.

The two girls continued to clean up the brown and black dog, stopping often to pat her head, letting her know that she'd be well taken care of. When they finished, they escorted her over to a large dog bed in the corner, where she reunited with her little puppies. Daisy inspected each one carefully. Satisfied with their condition, they rested together, relieved that their ordeal was over. Preoccupied with the arrival of this needy canine family, the understaffed shelter had no time to bother with us. After all, we were already designated to someone for care, eventually.

After a long while of waiting, a woman finally approached our cage. Most people had only paused briefly to comment on our situation, but she was looking at us more closely. Short grayish hair framed her kindly face. Her t-shirt matched Jennie and Sarah's, except it was faded with some minor fraying at the edging. Her warm, welcoming smile implied a soft tender heart. Opening the cage door she reached in, picking me up very gently. At first I hissed, letting her know I could fight if I needed to. "Stop that, you silly kitten," she chuckled, not threatened whatsoever.

Holding me close, she stroked my head softly. Somehow, instinct told me that she was a person that could be trusted. Melting in her arms I realized this was the affection I had yearned for. Automatically I began to purr, nuzzling against her.

"Well, aren't you friendly," she finally said. "My name is Judy. You're coming home with me. I already have the perfect family waiting for you once you have a clean bill of health and are ready for adoption."

Switching me for calico, she remarked, "Look at you, what a beautiful calico you are! It won't be hard finding a home for you either."

Not sure what to make of all this, calico became quiet, watching Judy carefully.

Fortunate to have only spent a few hours caged in a shelter, we left with Judy for her home. Calico and I remained very solemn during this our longest car ride yet. "We're here!" announced Judy, breaking the silence. "I've lots of new friends for you to meet."

Introductions began with a medium sized, sandy colored dog. "Say hello to my dog, Abby. She's very friendly. I'm sure you'll get along great," said Judy.

Further inside we encountered a litter of six young Labrador puppies and four older foster cats. High upon a climber we noticed a large black and white long haired cat sleeping soundly. This was Jake, a permanent resident. Accustomed to the comings and goings of many fosters animals, he could not be bothered interrupting his nap for greetings.

Our new quarters consisted of a small room with a gate in the doorway. Jumping the gate with ease, the other foster cats entered and exited the room at will. Too small yet to scale the gate, calico and I remained confined to our space. Through the enclosure, we could view the puppies across the hall experiencing similar circumstances. Our present accommodations provided us with all the essentials. Food, water, a soft bed and plenty of toys were at our disposal.

Dutifully, Abby positioned herself between us and the puppies, keeping a watchful eye. "You are two lucky kittens," she eventually said. "Judy will find you both good families and will take good care of you while you're here."

"What will happen to us now?" asked calico.

"Judy will take you to the doctor for shots and a check up. Once they decide you're healthy and old enough she will find you both homes," Abby answered.

"Will calico and I be able to stay together?" I asked, not sure I wanted an answer.

"Sometimes kittens get lucky and stay together. Don't get your hopes up though because this doesn't happen often. Sooner or later we all say goodbye to our siblings, but we get a family in exchange. It'll all be okay, don't worry," Abby truthfully replied.

Living with Judy, Abby had gained expertise in the area of fostering pets. For as long as she could remember there was a constant flow of kittens and puppies through her home. Grateful to have such a benevolent owner, she felt a responsibility to assist Judy with their care.

Abby explained to us that it's easier to place small kittens than grown cats. Most people seem to want a cute, tiny kitten. The older foster cats staying with Judy had many different stories. Some previously had families whose owners could no longer keep them. Another had special needs requiring particular arrangements. Sooner or later Judy would find the right home for all of them, it just took a little longer.

"Orange tabby, do you remember mom telling us that father had been in a foster home?" calico asked me.

"That's right, she did say that. Everything worked out well for dad, I'm sure we'll be fine. I just wish mother knew we were okay," I said with a sigh.

Reflecting upon what mother might be doing at this very moment, my mind drifted away slowly. I could picture her ambling aimlessly around with tears streaming from her bright, green eyes. Her heart must be broken, thinking that the worst had happened to us.

I saw her waiting outside of father's house, trying to get his attention with low pitched squeals. Looking out the window puzzled by her unprecedented presence, he signaled to her that he'd be out as soon as he had the chance. Patiently, she waited for him to be able to sneak away. Smokey and Oliver appeared at the window, staring naively at mother, they had no idea of the disturbing news she was about to deliver to them. At least she could take comfort in knowing that they were both safe and happy.

Mother debated whether or not it was in their best interest to tell them the truth about calico and me. Perhaps it would be better if they didn't know we'd been maliciously snatched away. What was taking father so long? She couldn't stand the wait any longer! She needed to talk to him now. She needed him to console her!

Just when she was about to lose her nerve to divulge to him our terrible fate, he rounded the corner with a happy-go-lucky expression upon his face. He slowed as he neared her. She'd been crying, he could tell. "What is it? What's wrong?" he asked.

Tears welled up in her eyes. Choked up, she couldn't speak. Immediately, he guessed it could only have something to do with us. "Where are calico and orange tabby? Are they okay?" he questioned.

She could only answer by bawling loudly. Running to her side, he whispered, "What has happened. You must try to tell me."

Mother could not look into his eyes. How could she tell him his children were missing? Looking at the ground, she began, sobbing all the while, "I left them for a minute, to get dinner. I told them to stay inside! When I got back they were far off in the yard!"

Father knew this story was only going to get worse. He started to weep as he listened patiently. Mother continued, "I saw a man creeping toward them. I screamed to warn them, but it was too late! He grabbed them from behind and threw them into a bag. There was nothing I could do! He took them away! I don't know what's happened to them! I'll never see them again!"

Mother was crying harder than ever now. Trying to be strong, father had no words. He could only share in her misery. They sat together for a very long time, before they were both worn out from grief. They agreed not to burden Oliver and Smokey with our tragedy. He'd make up a story of how she'd merely missed them and wanted a visit with father. With the knowledge that their lives would never be the same, they parted somberly, each to manage alone with heartache.

I can't bare this awful daydream any longer. I force myself to return my thoughts to the present situation with calico. What had Abby been saying? Oh, yes! She was telling us about our imminent adoptions.

Slowly the realization of our separate destinies began to sink in. Neither of us was prepared to discuss the reality bluntly unveiled by Abby. I chose not to speak of the inevitable for the time being, as to not upset calico unnecessarily.

Distracted from my thoughts by a meandering visit from Jake, my focus deviated. In contrast to Abby's helpful demeanor, Jake offered mere complacency.

Roaming through our room with an air of smugness, Jake halted for a time to look us over with an intimidating sneer. "Leave those kittens alone, Jake! They've been through enough without you bothering them" Abby barked at Jake.

Without uttering a word, Jake defiantly ate from our food bowl before turning to leave. Glaring at Abby he mumbled under his breath as he left, "They're just more kittens, nothing special…. Don't get so involved, Abby."

"Don't worry about Jake. He's been here longer than I have and thinks all of this is his domain. He feels we're all trespassing in his home. If you don't bother him, he won't bother you," Abby advised.

The disturbance caused by Abby's scolding of Jake provoked the puppies to bark excitedly. Alerted by the commotion, Judy came to check on the bunch. "What's all this noise about?" she questioned.

Noticing Jake slinking away, she understood. "Jake, have you been bothering the new kittens?" she said, folding her arms "Good girl," she said to Abby, petting her head. "You always look out for our fosters, don't you?"

Quieting down the puppies, she turned her attention to us. "Well now. Let's get a good look at you two. Looks like you could both use a good cleaning!" she said.

Starting with our ears, Judy washed us from head to paw. Refreshed and contented we felt assured we'd have no worries during our stay with her. The safe atmosphere of our present surroundings was a comfortable contrast to our previous living conditions under the shed. Settling in quickly, we were thoroughly enjoying our new world.

The days passed with ease due to the steady routine to which we soon became accustomed. Feeding and cleaning were Judy's priorities before leaving for work. Abby then responsibly guarded us in her absence. Indifferent to those around him, Jake pursued his own predictable routine.

Certain days, Judy remained at home with us. These were the days we could almost certainly expect visitors. Different people would arrive, choosing their puppy carefully. Rapidly dwindling, the litter was reduced before our eyes. One after another found a home until no more remained.

"Abby, when will I be adopted?" calico asked, encouraged by what she had witnessed. Memories of mother and our experiences were fading fast for calico. Adapting well, she was anxious to have a home and family of her own.

"Very soon! I've heard Judy speaking with someone for each of you. It won't be long now, maybe even tomorrow!" Abby informed us.

Aware my time with calico was coming to an end, I tightly curled up on the bed. Pretending to rest, preventing the excited calico from seeing me sad, I noticed my back foot was very close to my face. Instinctively, I began to suckle upon it, mimicking the nursing I had done with mother, not so very long ago. The gratifying pleasure transported me back to a time of pure bliss. Calm and contented, I drifted off into a brief sleep.

"Wake up, orange tabby," calico said, nudging me. I had barely rested before she rudely disturbed me. "Did you hear Abby? We may be going to our homes tomorrow, aren't you excited?" she asked.

"That means we won't be together anymore. I'll miss you," I said.

"I'll miss you too, but I'll know you're okay and cared for. Remember mom said she'd miss Smokey and Oliver, but she knew they'd have a family to love them," calico reminded me.

"How do you know for sure that we'll end up in homes with good people? Remember Daisy from the shelter? She'd been with owners who didn't take good care of her at all! They tied her to a tree and left her there with all those puppies!" I reminded her.

The spark instantly left her while she considered this grim possibility. "Oh. I hadn't thought about that! What if our new families aren't kind, orange tabby?" she questioned.

"If my new family turns out to be awful, I'll escape the first chance I get! You have to do the same, calico. It would be better to live outside, like mother, than with mean people!" I told her, feeling a little better now that we had some sort of a contingency plan.

Bouncing right back as always, calico countered, "You know, orange tabby, you worry too much! I'm sure Judy wouldn't send us to live with anyone bad!"

Of course, I hoped she was right. Saying good bye was more difficult for me than for calico. She was ready to move on. Letting go of her would be hard. I took the first step by saying as convincingly as possible, "That's true. Judy will find us both good homes, I'm sure. I can hardly wait for tomorrow."

CHAPTER 7

Adoption

My heart raced while Judy coddled calico and me in an effort to say her goodbyes privately. Regardless of how many adoptions she had previously arranged, she was always surprised by how attached she had become. "I'm going to miss you two sweet little kittens. You'll both have good homes, I promise. Finding homes for you means that space will open up for me to bring someone else in who needs help," she said, petting us one more time.

Taking a deep breath, Judy placed us in the carrier. "Well, let's get going. Come on, Abby," she said.

The ride home from the shelter would be easier with Abby's company. Judy had prearranged a meeting with the two families she had chosen to adopt us. Agreeing to meet at the shelter was the simplest for all involved. Together in the carrier, I knew this was my final opportunity to express my feelings to calico.

I began by saying, "Calico, I know you'll be happy in your new home. I'll think of you and remember all the time we've spent with each other. Don't ever forget me."

After licking my head, calico said, "I want you to look your best for your new family, orange tabby. I'll think of you too! I could never forget what a great brother you've been to me."

There was nothing more to say. Calico and I were ready to begin our new lives as house cats, as mother would've wanted. A growing enthusiasm slowly replaced the dread I'd felt for so long. Trusting in Judy's selection, I was prepared to meet my new family.

Recognizing the familiar parking lot, Abby barked repeatedly, indicating our arrival. "I know, Abby. You love your visits here, don't you?" asked Judy. Content to be at Judy's side, she proudly accompanied us in.

Several people were patiently waiting, gathered around the front desk. "There are your new families," Judy whispered into our carrier.

"I wonder which family I'll go with," calico thought out loud. The suspense was completely unsettling.

"Hi, gang," Judy said to the group. "Follow me into the other room and I'll show you the kittens."

Handing calico to a young woman, an instant connection was clear. My eyes fixated on calico, watching her face light up. "She's adorable, Judy!" the woman said, elated.

Showing calico to her husband they knew without words they had just found the perfect new member to their household. This young couple was obviously newlywed, not quite ready yet for the lifetime commitment of children. Adopting this kitten would, without doubt, begin their new family together. Calico would certainly become their beloved "baby".

Engrossed by calico's inspirational reception, I'd completely forgotten my turn was fast approaching.

Allowing calico to become better acquainted with her owners, Judy reached for me. "This kitten is a real sweetheart," she told the mom. "You'd think he'd be really afraid of people after all he's been through, but he's surprisingly loveable!"

Passing me to a tall, brown-haired teenage boy, this moment became more than I'd ever dreamt. Holding me against his soft, gray shirt, he stroked my head, not ever wanting to let me go.

"Well, hello!" he said. "You're so little. Would you like to come home with me? I promise to take good care of you!"

"What do you think, Ben?" asked his mother, already sure of his answer.

"He's definitely the one! Look at him. He's perfect!" confirmed Ben.

"You were right, Judy. You've found us another beautiful kitten. I know Ben will be very happy with him!" said his mom.

Ben was a large boy for fifteen, already towering over his mother. Despite his full grown size, he was especially gentle and compassionate. Looking on quietly was Ben's younger sister, Kayleigh. Her petite figure and long, blonde hair gave her quite an opposite look from that of her brother. It was difficult to believe by their appearance that these two were actually siblings.

Recently, she just had the opportunity to choose her own kitten. She had been promised a small kitten for Christmas. Having a great passion for animals, her parents thought is was time she had a pet of her own for which to care. To everyone's surprise, Ben, unpredictably, developed a strong attachment and interest in her new kitten. The family decided together that a companion for Kayleigh's kitten would be a good idea, plus provide a necessary pal for Ben.

Thrilled her kitten would soon have a friend she asked, "What are you going to call him, Ben?"

"Kaito, his name's Kaito," Ben said, certain this was the perfect name for him. "Can we take him home today?" he asked Judy.

"Absolutely," she answered. "Your mom just has to fill out the paperwork."

Completely absorbed by all of the attention, I gradually became aware of calico calling to me in the background. "Orange tabby! Orange tabby!" she was shouting.

Looking at her with a puzzled expression, she announced, "Did you hear him say your name's Kaito? You have a name!"

During the commotion I hadn't been listening. "My name's Kaito?" I repeated back to her. Nodding her head vigorously, calico showed her approval.

'Kaito', the name echoed in my mind, triggering my thoughts back to those of mother. Recalling her words the day Oliver and Smokey received their names, I could imagine her saying, "You have a name. You'll be okay, Kaito."

Huddled around me, Ben and Kayleigh were busy fussing over his new kitten. Mom stepped to the side for a quick phone call to Dad at work, including him in the excitement. "Wait until you see him," I heard her say. "He's really special!" This not quite yet middle-aged mother of two radiated a steady burst of vivacious energy. She expressed just as much enthusiasm over the adoption as both of her children.

Calico was thoroughly enjoying the affection the young couple was showering upon her.

Amidst this activity, I noticed Judy taking a moment to look on with a satisfied smile. Convinced she'd made the right decision, it was time to continue expediting the adoption process.

"If you're ready, all you need to do now is fill out the form and pay the fee," Judy said, interrupting.

The two women followed Judy to the counter. "Stay with Kaito, kids. I'll be right back," the mom said.

Returning instantly, the young woman loudly said to her husband across the room, "What's the name we decided on for her? I need to be sure for the paperwork."

After thinking for a minute, he answered, "I liked Maggie, isn't that what we agreed on?"

"You're right, I wasn't sure if that was it. We went over a lot of names!" she said, leaving the room again.

'Maggie', I liked it. It suited her, I thought. Before I could utter a word, calico was shouting to me, "My name's Maggie! Don't you love it, Kaito?"

Hesitating briefly before answering, I envisioned what mother's response would be. I then said, "Maggie is the most beautiful name I've ever heard. You have a name, Maggie. You'll be okay."

My statement brought a tear to her eye, knowing the sentiment it contained. For the rest of our days, we knew we could never forget the moment we started our new lives as Kaito and Maggie.

Abby diligently reported the progress of our adoptions to us. "They're almost finished. How's everything going here?" she inquired.

"Everything's great, Abby," said Maggie. "Thank you for taking such good care of us, we'll miss you."

Adding to Maggie's gratitude, I said, "You're a special dog, Abby. We'll always appreciate your help. Tell Jake we said good bye, he's really not so bad after all."

"I will," she replied. "You both take care of yourselves. I'll miss you too."

Returning shortly with the two women, Judy handed them each a card. "This has my phone number and e mail address. Send me an update once in while, letting me know how they are doing. I love to hear from my fosters," she said, hoping this wouldn't be the last time she'd ever see us.

Our time with Judy had reached an official end. With one last petting of our heads, she said her final goodbye. "Be good and be happy," were her last words to us.

"Don't worry," the woman said to Judy, "She'll be well taken care of and very loved!" Placing Maggie into her carrier, the woman said to her husband, "Come on. Let's take her home."

My heart thumped as they walked out the door, waving. The image of Maggie staring back at me through the bars would be forever imbedded into my memory. For the very first time, I was on my own.

"We should go too," said Ben's mom. "Ben, put Kaito in the carrier. You can hold onto it in the car on the way home."

Turning to Judy she said, "Thanks again, Judy. You know you'll be hearing from us. I'll send you lots of pictures of both kittens!"

"I know. I'll share them with the shelter. Take care," said Judy.

The transaction was complete. I was no longer the little orange tabby from under the shed. From now on I would be Ben's cat, Kaito.

CHAPTER 8

Home

The silver barred door squeaked open. Frightened to enter the outside freedom, I clung to the security of my pet carrier.

Invitingly, Kayleigh said, "Kaito, you can come out. This is your home. You're safe, it's okay."

"Give him a chance," snapped Ben, protectively. "He'll come out when he's ready. He's probably scared. Let's give him some space."

Normally, I required a prodding from Maggie to follow her adventurous lead. Relying upon my own instincts from now on, curiosity soon overtook my inhibitions. Cautiously, I approached the exit. Extending only a paw out the door, I remained prepared for a quick retreat. Allowing sufficient time to elapse, my guard significantly decreased.

"Look, Ben. You were right. Here he comes. Just give him a little more time to look around. Then show him where the food and litter are," Mom said.

Continuing to investigate my new surroundings, I found my new house to be impressive. No longer was I confined to a cage or limited to a single room. An entire house was now my personal territory. Two plump, oversized sofas lined the perimeter of the living area. Matching wooden tables neatly filled in the remaining spaces. An obviously well used reclining chair sat caddy cornered off to the side. Sparsely placed knick knacks decorated the room leaving a clean clutter-free space. There was so much to explore, it was overwhelming. While I was seeking a safe place to hide until I was ready to see more, Ben briskly intercepted me.

Gently picking me up, Ben whispered in my ear, "Well, Kaito, what do you think about all of this? It's been a big day for you, hasn't it?"

I wriggled a little in his arms, as he held me close against his warm chest. "This is the litter and here are your food and water." He placed me in front a large bowl filled with food and another with clean water.

Left standing on the cold, tiled floor, I looked around. A cozy place had been arranged in the spotless laundry room for my eating and litter box needs. There was a small, gray rug under the litter box entrance and a cat-shaped placemat beneath the food and water bowls. Sampling some dry cat food, I noticed the family monitoring me eagerly from the doorway. Feeling uncomfortable, I trotted out of the room, once again seized by Ben.

From the other room, a strange deep voice called out, "I'm home. Where's the new kitten?"

My ears perked up. I'd not heard this voice before. Who could this be? I watched the doorway intently.

"He's in here, Dad," Kayleigh yelled back.

Entering the room was a tall man in a dark, blue suit. His hair was buzzed into a crew cut. So short, that it was hard to notice any gray amidst the dark brown stubble. Remarkably, Ben resembled him in every way. There was no mistaking their relations. He'd left work early, primarily to welcome the newest member of his family, regretful that he wasn't able to be there for the actual adoption.

Taking me from Ben's arms to his own, Dad said smiling, "He's really cute, and so affectionate. I think you've made a good choice."

Dad's hands were rougher than Ben's. Clearly he worked hard around the house when he was not dressed in the fancy suit.

Uncontrollably purring, I adapted quickly to the lavish attention provided to me by my family. Closing my eyes, I envisioned a similar scenario occurring in Maggie's new home. Abby was right, we were two lucky kittens.

"He seems to be making himself right at home," Dad said. "You forgot to tell me he was an orange tabby. I love how his nose is split, half white and half orange."

"Oh. I thought I'd told you what he looked like when I called you," apologized Mom.

"I'm just thinking. He might just be right for the new ad we're doing for that pet store. He has the right temperament and his nose is unique for an orange tabby," he said, contemplating.

"Seriously, Dad?" shouted Ben. "You think they'd use him in an ad?"

"Why can't my kitten be in the ad?" yelled Kayleigh, enviously.

"Well," Dad began tactfully, realizing the sensitive position he was now in. "For one thing, your kitten is gray and the owner wanted an orange cat. Also, he is a little too shy; I think he'd be really scared. Kaito warms up quickly and has been through so much that all of the commotion of a camera shoot probably wouldn't even faze him."

Disappointed, she knew she couldn't argue the point. Resilient as always, she quickly decided to be happy for Kaito. "I understand. Can I go to watch Kaito at the photo shoot?" she asked, hoping Dad would be vulnerable enough to agree.

"I'll see what I can do," he said, with a wink.

Holding me up in the air, he looked me in the eye and asked, "How'd you like to be in an ad, Kaito?"

A little frightened and worn-out from the day's excitement, I managed to make a small squeak. Everyone laughed while Dad put me down carefully. "Why don't we introduce him to his new friend?" asked Dad.

"I'll go get him, Dad," volunteered Kayleigh anxiously.

My attention was drawn to Kayleigh dashing from the room. Who was this new friend I was about to meet? Watching the doorway, apprehensively, I awaited her return.

"Kaito, we have a surprise for you," announced Ben.

Placing a gray and white kitten before me, Kayleigh said, "Kaito, meet my kitten, Scooter."

Our eyes met. Struck with the same expression of disbelief, we inspected one another thoroughly. Immediately, his appearance reminded me of mother and Smokey. Although he was noticeably larger than I, his unassuming demeanor suggested a timid disposition. Again, my thoughts drifted back, now to Oliver.

His familiar resemblance led to an instant fondness. Anticipating a special friendship, I chose to be assertive. Initiating the conversation, I proudly said, "Hi, my name is Kaito."

Obviously unprepared for such a meeting, Scooter took a moment before replying. Until now he had enjoyed complete attention from the entire family along with sole claim to the house. Wondering whether or not he would be willing to share his kingdom, I patiently waited for him to speak.

Following an awkward silence, to my relief he finally remarked, "Hi, Kaito! I wasn't expecting a new friend. I'm glad you're here."

"How long have you lived here?" I asked, attempting to become better acquainted.

"Almost two months," he said.

The family eagerly watched as we developed the beginnings of our new friendship.

"Well," commented Mom. "They seem to like one another! That's good. Scooter needs company when he's home alone. I'm glad that you decided you wanted a kitten too, Ben."

Kayleigh and Ben continued to play with us for a very long time. There were mice to chase, feathers on strings to catch and even a crinkly tunnel to hide in for optimal pouncing. Despite the great amount of fun we were having, we all eventually began to tire. One by one the family soon disbanded.

Searching for a quiet place to rest, I spotted a fuzzy blue blanket draped across the large couch. This location looked quite appealing. Choosing to nap here, I purred while kneading the fuzzy blanket, circling around and around until it felt just right.

I reverted back to the comforting position discovered at Judy's, enabling me to suck upon my back foot as though I were nursing; it had become habitual. Simulating mother's nurturing brought back soothing thoughts with a calming effect. Parting with mother so abruptly, I feared, was a trauma from which I might never completely recover.

Unaware of Scooter curiously observing my ritual, I was slightly startled when he suddenly blurted out from the top of the couch, "Kaito, why are you sucking on your foot like that?"

Debating my response, I decided a brief explanation would be best. "I daydream that my mother is with me. It helps me to go to sleep," I answered honestly.

"Where's your mom now?" inquired Scooter. "Didn't you give her a big good bye? I like to think of how happy my mom was for me the day I was adopted. She knew we'd all have good lives."

Apparently, Scooter was not going to be satisfied until he heard the entire story. Taking a deep breath, I proceeded to explain to him all the events that led to my present circumstances. Beginning with the shed, I described mother, father, and my siblings. Then I explained how dad brought Smokey and Oliver to live with him.

Scooter was listening with wide eyes as I told him how Maggie and I were snatched that day, right in front of mother, leaving her wailing in despair. Reliving our terrifying experience swelled my eyes up with tears. Seeing my pain, Scooter interrupted, "You don't have to tell me what happened if it's too upsetting. I understand."

"No. It's good to talk about it." I said continuing. "A girl found us in a dumpster. She took care of us until she brought us to Judy."

"Judy!" exclaimed Scooter. "The Judy with Abby and Jake?"

Scooter's enthusiasm was contagious. "Yes!" I shouted back. "Do you know Judy?"

"I lived with Judy from the day I was born until I was adopted. I didn't know you were with Judy too! How's Abby?" questioned Scooter.

"Abby's great! It was wonderful staying there," I said.

Having Judy in common helped Scooter and me to bond quickly. Obviously, Scooter's experience had been very different from my own. I wondered, to myself, what it would've been like to have had more time with mother.

Would it have been easier if I'd had the chance to tell her good bye, her knowing I'd be all right?

CHAPTER 9

Scooter's Tale

It was clear, Scooter and I were not going to get much sleep that first night. We were both eager to hear the other's story. Our backgrounds had been quite different. Scooter had always enjoyed the warmth and comfort of the indoors. He had been surrounded by only love and kindness, just as father had been. He'd never known fear or heartache, giving him an open, gentle heart.

"I have four siblings," he began. "One is an orange tabby, like you. Then there's my calico sister and two other gray and white kittens, like me."

"What about your mother?" I interrupted, anxious to know what she was like.

"I'm getting to her," he said, losing his train of thought for a moment. "My mother's name is Elise. She is a beautiful all-gray cat. A woman found her near her office one night. Mom was pregnant with us and very friendly. The woman called Judy, who took her in."

"You were born in Judy's house?" I asked. This meant his mother was free to care for her babies without worry. They did not have to hide in a dark, dirty place or huddle together to keep warm during the long, cold nights. Grasping the realm of comforts that began Scooter's life was incomprehensible to me. Worrying about our safety and well being was a constant concern for my mother.

I had to know more about his mother. "Did you say your mother's name is Elise? Do you know what happened to her?" I pursued.

"Mother told us that once we'd all found good homes Judy was going to find her a home too," he said.

Then and there I understood, really understood; why mother found it so important that Smokey and Oliver were named. She knew that once a cat was named it was no longer just a cat, but a pet. A pet became part of a family. With the occasional exception, most people who owned a pet expressed a special love and affection for it. All people have names, and when they name a cat or dog, suddenly they become part of that world. Mother was wise to realize this.

Scooter's mother was fortunate to have a name and to know her kittens were all being named. I wish more than anything that I was able to give my mother that same peace of mind. If only she knew my name was Kaito, then I might not long for her so greatly.

Deep in thought with this latest epiphany, I had stopped listening to Scooter's story. "Kaito!" he shrieked. "Have you heard what I was saying?"

"I'm sorry," I apologized, sincerely. "I was thinking of my mother. So, how did you end up here?" I said, trying to pay closer attention.

Sighing, to show his annoyance, he reluctantly retold his experience of his adoption day. "One day mother told us that this was the day we were all to find homes. She was so proud of her beautiful litter. One by one she gave us a special grooming, showing us how much we were loved. Then we said our good byes," he recounted.

"Were you very sad?" I wondered.

"No. We were all going to homes. We were happy to find families," he assured me.

Scooter was having difficulty staying on track with his story with my constant interruptions. He was being patient, but I decided I shouldn't bother him with more diversions.

"Anyway," he said. "Judy put us all into the carrier, taking us to the shelter. There were a lot of families waiting to see us. I noticed a young girl. She looked very kind. I kept walking over to her, making her pick me up."

"I think he likes you," her mother said to her. "What do you think about him?"

"I really like him," she replied. "Can I have him?"

"Well, I guess you've made your choice," she said. Turning to Judy, she announced, "We'll take this one, Judy."

"After filling out the paperwork, I went home with Kayleigh. I've been happy here ever since," he concluded.

"Wow!" I commented. "She picked you for her kitten, out of the whole litter!"

"Weren't you listening, again?" he rebuffed. "I picked her! A lot of times the people think they have chosen a pet, but really we have picked them."

"I didn't know that," I said. I had thought Ben picked me, but I suppose if I hadn't liked him I would've acted unfriendly so he wouldn't take me. Without knowing it, I guess I'd chosen this family.

Scooter's story had given me a lot to think about. Having never been someone's pet, mother hadn't been able to instruct me on what to expect. Scooter had the advantage of preparation. Following his lead to fit into this family was my new strategy.

The night had been long and draining. Completely exhausted by daybreak, I repeated my foot sucking ritual, swiftly falling to sleep. The family had slowly begun to stir, initiating their morning routine.

"I heard those kittens all night," complained Mom. "Now they decide to go to sleep. I hope they sleep tonight!"

"Mom, look at Kaito's foot. It's all wet," commented Ben.

"Huh," said Mom, perplexed. "He must've been sucking on his foot, like a baby sucks its thumb."

"Why would he do that?" Kayleigh questioned.

"Remember Judy told us that he was thrown into a dumpster. I'll bet he left his mother too soon and wasn't weaned properly," Mom determined.

Sympathetically looking at me curled up on the blue blanket with one wet foot, Mom said softly to me, "Poor baby, do you miss your mother? I'm so sorry for you." She gently stroked my head. I opened my eyes enough to see the compassion in her expression. They understood me. Our special bond had truly begun.

CHAPTER 10

Fame

The front door flew open, a rush of cold, brisk air followed Dad in. Before he ventured to take off his coat, he impatiently called out to the family. "I'm home! Where is everyone! I've got news!" he shouted.

Speeding to the foyer in record time, Mom, Ben and Kayleigh arrived to observe Dad wrestling vigorously with his coat.

"Okay, Dad. We're here. What's going on?" Ben questioned, puzzled.

"Great news!" he said, with a dramatic pause just long enough to completely grab everybody's attention. Dad had a special knack for captivating his audience while telling a story. Everyone, it seemed, always stopped and listened whenever he spoke.

With their jaws dropped and eyes wide open, they listened to him deliver his breaking news bulletin. "I spoke with the pet store owner, Mr. Biggleton. Kaito is in! They're using him for their ad!" he proudly announced.

"No way!" Ben blurted out. "I can't believe it! I knew he was special!"

"Awesome!" exclaimed Kayleigh. "Can I…"

"Yes!" Dad interrupted, knowing precisely what she was about to ask. "You can go. We can all go to watch the shoot!"

"That's amazing! How did you ever convince that crabby old man to use our Kaito?" Mom inquired. She was always curious about the details.

"It was easy, actually. I told him all about Kaito. I showed him his picture and Mr. Biggleton agreed right away. Maybe I caught him in a good mood, for once!" Dad joked.

Oblivious to the plans for my future fame, I innocently trotted into the room to investigate the lively uproar.

"Kaito! How'd you know we were talking about you?" laughed Ben, noticing me at his feet.

"Come here, buddy," said Dad. Picking me up, he briefly looked me over. "We have to be there early enough this Saturday for them to give him a good grooming," reported Dad.

The excitement mounted all through the week leading up to that eventful day. Dad's work in advertising had always been somewhat interesting, but now that the whole family was caught up in the frenzy, it was completely intriguing.

Going about my business as usual, I couldn't fathom what had the family so frazzled that week. The anticipation of the approaching photo shoot caused everyone to be just a little edgy.

At last, the remarkable day arrived. The morning sun had just begun to shine through the streaky kitchen windows as the family hustled to get ready.

"Do I look all right in this outfit?" Kayleigh asked anyone who was not too busy to answer.

"No one is taking your picture! Who cares how you look," replied Ben curtly.

"I wasn't talking to you, Ben!" she rightfully yelled back.

"Okay, enough already, both of you. Kayleigh, you look fine. Ben, grab Kaito and let's get going!" said Mom, restoring order.

Into the carrier I went hurriedly. The door closed and locked even before I had a chance to turn myself around. Where were we going? This behavior was much too suspicious for an ordinary trip to the vet. Peering out from under the couch, I noted Scooter looking on nervously.

Before I could guess what was happening we were in the car, driving up the street. Fearful of what was to come next, a sudden panic arose. Mewing pathetically from the carrier, my protest was not taken lightly. Mom, removing me from the carrier, held me tightly against her.

"Don't be scared, Kaito. You're just going for a picture. You're perfectly safe!" she said, attempting to comfort me. What did she mean a picture?

My imagination began to take over. Maybe they changed their minds about me. What if they only wanted one cat and were taking me back? Would Judy take me back or would I end up in that confining cage in the shelter, this time alone, without Maggie?

The idea of being all alone scared me more than anything else. At least before Maggie and I were together. I could just see myself, alone shuddering in the corner of a cold, hard cage. Different people would come by, looking me over. My trust for humans would never be the same. What if a person took me who wasn't kind? I trembled with fear imagining the countless possibilities.

Closing my eyes, I cuddled with Mom as closely as I could. "Please take me back home," I begged her. "I want to stay with all of you and Scooter!"

Speaking quietly, for Dad's ears only, Mom whispered, "I hope he doesn't act so frightened when we get there, or they're not going to want to use him. The kids will be really disappointed. They're so excited about this."

"Let's just hope for the best. I'm sure he'll warm up," Dad said, trying to persuade himself. Mr. Biggleton definitely wouldn't be happy if the kitten Dad had recommended didn't work out.

We rode the rest of the way in silence. Turning sharply from the main road, we entered a half empty parking lot behind an unimpressive two story, red brick building. Purposefully parking an adequate distance from the other vehicles to help ensure Dad's new car was safe from careless drivers, he casually announced our timely arrival, "We're here."

"Here? Where's here?" I thought to myself. This certainly wasn't the shelter where Judy worked. Why did they ever bring me here? Voluntarily scooting back to the security of my trusty, old carrier, I kept trying to convince myself that no harm would come to me. Be brave, Kaito! Think of Maggie. She wouldn't be scared if she were here. It would all just be another exciting adventure to her.

We exited the car with the sound of four doors consecutively slamming shut and echoing while we darted across the seemingly endless parking lot. Dad took hold of my carrier as though he were running in a relay race. Thrashing around inside, I attempted to steady myself.

"Follow me! We're right on time. Through those doors and make a left," he commanded using a new business-like tone.

Stopping short, he paused to look around briefly before spotting a short, pudgy woman signaling to him. Like well-trained ducklings, the family automatically fell in line behind Dad.

"Hi, Mr. R.!" Peering into the carrier, she asked in an an irritating nasal voice, "Is this our star?"

"How are you, Peggy?" he replied. They had worked together before on different assignments. Although he found her to be somewhat annoying, she was one of the best in her field. Initiating proper introductions Dad said, "Yes, this is Kaito. This is my wife, Michelle, and kids, Ben and Kayleigh."

"Nice to meet you," she said to them, taking the time to shake hands with each one. "Please excuse me while I get Kaito into grooming. Grab a seat and make yourself at home."

The cage door squeaked open, her icy cold hand reached in, grabbing me by the scruff of the neck. "Come on, little guy. You'll be okay," she squawked.

Sensing my fear from the look of desperation in my eyes, Ben jumped to his feet, "Would I be able to go with him? I think he's scared. I don't want him to think we're abandoning him or something," Ben implored.

"Sure. Why not?" Peggy nonchalantly answered back.

Warm water trickled down my back as she dangled me under a shiny silver faucet. Bathing did not upset me whatsoever given that Judy had cleaned me in this manner numerous times. Oddly, I had come to quite enjoy a good washing. Peggy proceeded to give me a first-class scrubbing, lathering me up in a froth of soapy suds.

Ben vigilantly watched over me, concerned that I may become frightened. "That crazy cat seems to actually like having a bath," he commented in disbelief.

Using a soft, fluffy, white towel she carefully patted down my dripping wet fur before I had the opportunity to instinctively shake dry. Peggy delicately cleaned out my ears with several oversized spongy q-tips. This rather pleasant experience caused me to quite forget my old fears.

"You're right, Ben. Kaito seems to love his grooming. He has a perfect temperament," Peggy said, diligently continuing with her task.

By utilizing a tiny brush, each tooth was individually polished to a sparkling shine. A final fluff of warm air from a blow dryer finished the look.

"Wow, Kaito, do you ever look handsome!" exclaimed Ben. "You smell good too. No more fishy breath either."

"He does look stunning, if I do say so myself," Peggy said, taking full credit for a job well done.

I was immediately rushed into an exceedingly well lit area and stood there astounded, gazing at all that was around me. A few moments were needed to become accustomed to the hot, bright lights that shone directly upon me. Squinting as my eyes adjusted to the intense lighting I became aware of a small group of people looking straight at me. Now who are they, I wondered?

Under my paws lay a squishy, green carpet resembling the grass from the outside of our shed. Behind me, a gigantic blue screen riddled with wispy white clouds created a genuine feeling of being outdoors. Feeling playful, I scampered and pounced without a worry. A murmur of whispering was coming from the small crowd. Some had big cameras, snapping pictures non stop.

A whiff of an incredibly familiar scent suddenly caught my attention, stopping me right in my tracks. There before me sat a sparkling, crystal dish filled with a mouth-watering display of what appeared to be tuna, my absolute favorite!

Pangs of hunger reminded me that somehow breakfast was overlooked this morning.

All eyes watched me cautiously approach the bowl. First a sniff, then a lick, I was right. It was tuna! I dove into this delicious meal as though I hadn't eaten in a month, lights flashing continually around me.

Every part of of this attentive pampering rapidly went to my head, causing me to believe I'd become a sudden celebrity. Imagining Dad bringing me out through the back exit with the crowds of fans waiting just to catch a glimpse of me, Kaito the superstar, began a fantastic daydream.

A sparkling collar encircled with dazzling gems lies elegantly around my neck. An expensive pair of coordinating designer sunglasses compliments my new look perfectly. My old, dull carrier will no longer do. A polished, golden, wired enclosure provides my countless admirers a better opportunity to see me. The bottom of my new mode of transport is lined with a silky, soft, snow-white cushion, offering me ultimate comfort while traveling.

This was indeed the privileged life I'd only dreamt about while living beneath the shed with mother. Had she known about my newly found success, her pride would surely be overflowing.

Closing my eyes, I could hear her words as if she were standing right beside me, "Kaito, I always knew you were destined for greatness. Perhaps we do have royal bloodlines after all for you to have become such a regal cat!"

Yes, this is the good life, I thought to myself, deeply immersed in this blissful fantasy. Just then, quite abruptly the bright lights shut off. Looking around, I realized that the pack of fans had also left, leaving only irritating Peggy looking over me. Perhaps they had gone off to prepare for my big debut, I concluded refusing to be discouraged.

Smiling cheerfully, Ben and Dad soon approached me. "Great job, Kaito! You're the best kitten ever!" boasted Ben.

"Okay, time to go back home now, you've had quite a day," Dad added. He set down the old, shabby carrier in front of me. Did he actually think a star of my quality was going to ride in that rundown thing? And where were my new collar and sunglasses?

"Go ahead in," urged Ben. This is not acceptable, I thought. I was not budging until my new golden carrier arrived!

"What's his problem?" questioned Dad.

"I think he's had too much fun and doesn't want to go," said Peggy. "Kaito, did you like having all that attention?" she said to me, patting my head forcefully with those still frozen hands.

Scooping me up carefully into his large hands, Dad attempted to place me right into that sub-standard carrier. Reluctantly I entered, only after squirming sufficiently enough to show my protest.

"I don't know what's gotten into you, Kaito, but it's time to go back home," he bluntly informed me.

Eventually the harsh realization that I hadn't risen to stardom gradually sunk in. There were no crowds waiting outside to greet me. No dazzling gems or fancy new carrier. Disappointed, I remained solemn during the long trip home. Quite the opposite was true for the family, however.

"Everyone thought Kaito was just the cutest kitten ever," Kayleigh bragged.

"He did an awesome job, all of the crew thought so. When will his picture be on the ad, Dad?" asked Ben.

Resting his head against his hand with his arm leaning in the window of the car door, Dad took in a deep breath.

"Well," he began, "There's a process. First, they have to agree on the picture they like the best. Then they…"

Interrupting as only she could, Mom chimed in impatiently, "We really don't need to know the whole drawn out process. Just tell us approximately how many weeks it will take until we can buy the food with his picture on the package."

"Six to eight weeks," he answered, obviously offended.

"Thanks, honey. Sorry for cutting you off in your story," Mom apologized. Giving Dad a small peck on the cheek, she whispered tenderly into his ear. At once all was well again. He never could stay mad with her.

Before long the exhilaration from the day's events soon wore off leaving one and all worn-out and tired. The soothing music from Dad's favorite oldies CD played softly in the background during the remaining trip back home.

Dusk was fast approaching as we finally arrived home. As we meandered listlessly from the car into the house, our adventurous day had come to a close. A concerned Scooter sat nervously by the front door bursting with questions.

Full of energy, he charged at me rapidly firing one question after another not allowing enough time for any answering. "Where were you? Why were you gone so long? What happened? I didn't know if you were coming back! Why do you smell different? Who did you see today? Well?"

Waiting for him to run out of steam before venturing a response I debated if he would believe the truth about the day's events. Choosing to take the risk, I opted to be honest and tell him the entire story.

Scooter attentively listened to me recalling the highlights from the day. A second wind came over me as I described in detail about Peggy, the grooming and all of the crew busily snapping pictures.

Fascinated, Scooter sought after even more information. "Were you scared, Kaito?" he wanted to know.

Of course I didn't want to admit to him that I'd been an absolute crybaby the whole way there. What could it hurt to let him believe I was brave and fearless?

"What's there to be afraid of? My family wouldn't let anything happen to me. It was all a fun adventure!" I coolly replied.

Hearing my own words, I realized how silly it was to have been so frightened. They really did love me. Deep down I guess I'd known they were always going to take good care of me.

It no longer seemed to matter that I wasn't royal or a big celebrity. Having a family that loves and cares for me is far more important than a flashy new collar. Scooter and I were fortunate to live together in such comfort without any worries. Appreciating the good life of an ordinary housecat, I'd be sure to savor every moment from now on.

CHAPTER II

Surprise

"Come on, Kaito," said Dad. "I know that look in your eye by now."

Placing my fuzzy blue blanket across his lap, Dad signaled me to jump up. I had become quite predictable with my desire to curl up to suck upon my back foot.

"Okay, buddy. I know you need your foot sucking time," he repeated.

Compulsively, I leaped up onto his lap. First kneading and then turning around until finally I settled into a familiar position. Dad softly stroked my head while I dozed off, my wet foot still partly in my mouth.

Passing through the room, Mom paused for a moment to comment. Shaking her head with a smile, she remarked, "That cat's over three years old and he still sucks on his foot like a baby. I guess he'll never grow out of it." Moving closer to us, she bent down. Looking into my face she gently whispered, "Kaito, it's what makes you a very special cat."

Everyone understood, accepting my quirky habit as unique. Even Scooter tolerated my infantile behavior.

Occasionally, he silently looked on, pondering the absurdity of a thirteen- pound, three-year-old cat sucking his foot, still thinking of his mother.

The truth be told, I did still think of my mother. Although I couldn't have imagined a better life or family, my mother's memory always remained with me.

After a restful foot-sucking induced sleep, I joined Scooter by the back door. "Anything yet?" I asked, hoping he saw something out there.

"No!" he answered restlessly.

A set of all-glass french doors provided the perfect place for us to sit for a vantage point of the entire backyard. From there we were able to watch the birds and squirrels scurrying through our yard in complete comfort and safety.

Suddenly, sighting some birds, we crouched down low, only the tops of our heads remained visible. "Get down!" Scooter commanded. "Don't let them see us."

"Okay, be still," I replied.

Separated from the outdoors by a mere piece of glass, our presence obviously posed no threat to their existence.

"If this door were open, I'd pounce on you birds and catch you," Scooter boasted, loud enough for the birds to hear.

Determined to mock our confinement, blatantly, the birds pranced within a normally dangerous proximity. Knowing this reality did not prevent us from pretending to be great hunters.

Never tiring from this activity, Scooter and I spent numerous hours gazing out the door, waiting for one of these feathery creatures to happen upon our yard.

Occasionally, a new and unusual animal would mysteriously appear outside our door. If we were lucky, and waited patiently, we would catch a rare glimpse of a opossum or skunk meandering home from a long night of scavenging.

The excitement from such a sight encouraged us to stand watch often.

No longer young kittens, Scooter and I now tire quite easily, causing us to alternate between activities and long, frequent naps. Content with eating, sleeping, and window gazing, we have enjoyed little disruption in routine throughout the years we have spent with our family. Pleasantly, we have all fallen into a very comfortable schedule.

"Let's have our final patrol for the night before going to bed," insisted Scooter this evening.

Generally agreeable, I accepted, "Okay, let's take another look."

Feeling especially sleepy, my enthusiasm and expectations were somewhat lacking during this particular round. Fortunately, Scooter had enough eagerness for both of us, picking up the slack.

Perking up abruptly, Scooter appeared alarmed. "Did you see that?" he asked.

"See what? Where?" I answered. My interest had been instantly revived.

"There it is again!" he shouted.

This time I too saw. The absence of daylight made it difficult to distinguish what creature we had actually spotted. Looking intently through the glass, we decided to remain where we were until a determination was made.

The silhouette of this animal was surprisingly familiar. Yet, this was certainly not a sight we had seen before.

Following a short silence, Scooter whispered in disbelief, "Kaito, I think that is a cat, like us."

Stunned, so many questions ran through my mind. Where had it come from? What was it doing in my yard? Did it think it was going to stay? Finally, all I could manage to reply was, "I think you are right, Scooter!"

Diligently, Scooter and I remained steadfast on our quest to get another glimpse of the elusive intruder. Positioned perfectly for optimal viewing we lay in wait, deep into the night. We kept ourselves low, with only our nose and above visible from the outside, so as not to be seen by the stranger. Detecting not even the slightest motion for an eternity, it was becoming evident that this cat was not reappearing tonight. Steadily we were growing weary, our initial enthusiasm fading rapidly.

With a yawn big enough to show all of his teeth, Scooter managed to mutter, "I'm too tired to keep up the watch. Let's go to bed and try again tomorrow, Kaito."

"Okay." I agreed without hesitation.

My recollection of what came next was blurred by my complete exhaustion. My dreams were filled with visions of what we had just witnessed, as I'm sure were Scooter's.

A restless night quickly led to an early morning rise. Memories of the stranger flooded my consciousness as my eyes were struggling to open. Leaping to my feet, while remaining in a state of half sleep, I staggered dutifully to the back door. Not surprisingly, Scooter had beaten me to our post.

"Good morning, Kaito!" he said, annoyingly awake and ready for the day.

"Morning," was all I was able to grunt back at him.

"I haven't seen anything yet, but I'm sure we'll catch that cat in our yard today," Scooter rambled, overly optimistic. I just nodded, indicating my desire to delay any conversation until I was more awake.

Following us into the kitchen, shortly thereafter, was Mom, as usual the first one up. Noticing our exuberant interest with the backyard, she ritually prepared her mug of morning coffee. She casually joined our surveillance and asked, "So, what have you boys spotted out there that has you so interested? Let's hope it's not that horrible skunk again!"

Her words had barely left her mouth when simultaneously we all saw it! Prancing through our yard was the uninvited cat! What a spectacle! Gasping, Mom shouted, "Oh no! Where did that cat come from? So that's what has you two glued to the glass! Good job, boys!"

Scooter and I locked our eyes onto this stranger, determined not to lose sight of him. It was no wonder it was hard to identify him last night. This cat was solid black with one speck of white on his chest. Apparently unaware that he was being watched, he was nonchalantly making his way under the gap of the fence. We did not know what to make of this new situation. Even Scooter was speechless.

Mom, however, had plenty to say. "I wonder what he was doing back there?" she began. "Maybe he's living behind the pool heater. I'm going to take a look back there and see what's going on," she stated, putting down her coffee and slipping into her old shoes.

Shooing us away from the door, Mom trampled through the wet grass to her destination as though she were on a serious mission. When she reached the pool heater she stopped suddenly and raised her hands to her face in surprise.

"What does she see, Kaito?" Scooter asked. The suspense was torturing us. We had to know what was there!

"I don't know, but look out! She's coming back fast!" I said, now wide awake!

Kicking off her shoes as she entered the back door, Mom raced to the closet retrieving our cat carrier. We had come to know that this was never good news. It always meant a scary trip to the vet which was generally accompanied by a shot. Cowering away at the sight of the carrier, Scooter and I hid under the table.

"Relax, boys! This isn't for you," she said reassuringly. "There are kittens back there and I've got to get them before the mother comes back, or we'll have real problems."

Abruptly, she once again shooed us away and continued on her quest to capture these kittens. Just then, Dad entered, joining the commotion already in progress. He was trying to piece together the situation, all the while mumbling to himself. "Hmm!" he began. "What in the world is she doing out there by the pool heater? It looks like she has the cat carrier. What could possibly be out there?" he wondered aloud.

Dad, Scooter and I watched speechlessly as Mom trudged back to the house. Once inside, she looked at Dad and told him, "You'll never believe it! I've caught three kittens in the yard. The mom ran away. You'll have to set the have-a-heart trap later so we can catch her too. She'll need to be fixed and taken to the shelter, if she is friendly."

Taking a moment to process this surprising information, Dad finally asked the obvious question we were all thinking, "What are we doing with these kittens?"

Not having thought this through, Mom scrunched her face and began her wheels turning. "Well, I keep in touch with Judy occasionally, perhaps I'll call her and she'll have a suggestion."

That was that! A decision had been made on what to do next. In the meantime, Mom and Dad put the little kittens into a big box in the corner, instructing us not to bother them. My curious personality led me to investigate. Scooter soon followed suit.

We peeked into the box slowly. They were so little and scared. Watching them huddle together for safety, memories of my own experiences immediately rushed back. Even though years had passed, it suddenly seemed like only yesterday.

CHAPTER 12

Reunion

The doorbell rang, instantly signaling my heart to beat faster with anticipation. Startled, Scooter jumped to his feet, eagerly awaiting the appearance of the visitor.

"I've got it!" bellowed Mom from the other room.

Then, before my very eyes, there she was just as I had remembered. She hadn't changed a bit over these past few years, although I'm sure Scooter and I looked quite different.

Always happy to have a chance to show us off, Mom said, "You remember Scooter and Kaito. They're a little bigger and a little older since you saw them last."

"Boys," she said turning to us. (Mom always referred to us as 'The Boys'), "Come say hello to Judy. Do you remember Judy?"

How could I forget! I never thought I'd have the chance to see Judy again! Running to her, I stopped at her ankles zig zagging through her feet, belting out my loudest purr.

Scooping me up, she pet my head and said, "Hello, Kaito! Still friendly I see. Wow! Did you ever get big?"

Being reunited with Judy was such an unexpected pleasure. Through my purring and cuddling I earnestly attempted to thank her. "Thank you, Judy, for the care you took of Maggie and me. Thank you for the family you found for my friend Scooter and me." I couldn't imagine where I'd have been without her.

"I'm glad you're happy, Kaito," she whispered into my ear, as if she knew just what I was trying to tell her.

The ever cautious Scooter watched from a safe distance. He was never keen on visitors in our house. Mom kindly referred to him as her shy cat.

"Come say hi, Scooter," I encouraged. "You know Judy, this is no time to be shy!"

Slowly he approached Judy, close enough for her to pet him, but ready to run if an attempt was made to pick him up. "Still a little skittish, Scooter?" Judy said as she gently pet his head. "That's okay, I won't pick you up."

"I think they remember you," Mom commented, observing our friendly behavior. "Did you bring Abby?"

"No. She's getting older and tires easily. I let her stay home to rest." Judy said, quickly changing the subject. "So, where are these kittens?"

Leading her into the kitchen, Mom showed Judy to the box. There, huddled together, were Judy's newest fosters.

Picking up the smallest of the litter, Judy carefully inspected the gray and white kitten before remarking, "They are about five weeks old. This one is a girl. They're very cute; it shouldn't be difficult placing them. Once you catch the mom, bring her to my house and I'll see what I can do for her."

Mom and Judy sat at the table for a quick cup of coffee, discussing the kittens. Hearing the soft cries of the fearful babies, I snuck over to the box, undetected by Mom. Peering into the box, I told them not to be afraid.

The little one that Judy held looked up at me and cried out, "Where's our mom? What will happen to us?"

"Don't worry! When I was little like you, I lost my mom too. Judy took my sister and me in and took really good care of us. She even found us wonderful families. She'll take care of you too. You'll love it at her house and you'll love Abby, her dog."

It felt strange to be the one delivering the comforting words. It was not so long ago that I was on the receiving end, not sure of what was happening to me. I was happy to be able to use my experiences to help these little ones.

Remembering the words that once consoled me, I spoke to them from my heart, "You're lucky kittens. Sometimes kittens get adopted together, but if you don't it'll be okay."

"Are you sure we'll be okay? How do you know?" they questioned me.

I thought for only a few moments before giving them the best answer I could, "You'll know that everything will be fine the moment you're given a name. You'll know then that you'll be taken care of and you'll be happy."

I know they couldn't understand just what I meant at this moment, but would come to see for themselves before long.

My time with them came to a rapid end as Judy and Mom approached with the carrier. Only having moments to say goodbye, I concluded our talk by saying, "Trust me, everything will work out fine. My name is Kaito and my friend is Scooter. Soon you'll have a name and a family too! Please do me a favor and tell Abby hello and thank you from us."

Being placed into the carrier, they called back, "We will! Thank you, Kaito; you've made us feel a lot better."

After a brief goodbye from Judy, they were off. Sitting in the quiet, Scooter and I took a minute to reflect on the day's events. We hadn't had that much excitement in years. It was a lot to absorb.

"They'll be fine," Scooter finally said, reassuringly.

"I know," I replied. Then all of the sudden it occurred to me! What about the mom in the yard! "Scooter, we have to look outside for their mom!"

Racing to the door, we panned the yard hoping to detect her. Sooner or later she'd return, we were sure of it. We'd wait all day if we had to.

Eventually, we were right. Traipsing back into the yard, oblivious to the happenings of the day, was the mom. We watched in suspense to see her reaction when she realized her litter was missing. Her howl was identical to that of my mother's so many years ago. Instinctively, the fur down my back raised in distress. She proceeded to call out for them, in hopes that they had only disobeyed and wandered.

Tapping our front paws on the window, Scooter and I frantically attempted to capture her attention. Finally, she turned and stared at us with a strong curiosity. Motioning her to come closer, we were relieved to be able to help her.

Face to face at the glass, all animosity towards this stranger instantly turned to sympathy and friendship. Easing her pain was our utmost priority.

"Who are you? Have you seen my kittens?" she shouted with desperation.

"I'm Kaito. They've been taken to foster care. A good woman named Judy has them and I can assure you she's taking excellent care of them," I answered.

Hanging her head low, she thanked us for the information. Her eyes were welling up with sadness, not being able to say her goodbyes.

"Wait!" I shouted. "I have an idea! Judy told Mom that if she could catch you, she should take you to Judy and Judy would find you a home for you, if you liked people."

She straightened up and a hopeful grin replaced her tears. "I do like people. I used to have a home, but the family moved and left me. What should I do to get to this Judy?"

The plan was simple. "They've set a trap over there by the pool heater. All you have to do is go in it and act friendly when you see Judy," I instructed her.

"I'll do it. Thank you, Kaito. You're a true friend," she said, gratefully.

She turned from our window, proceeding to the trap with a real purpose. We knew we would not see her again. It was gratifying to have helped her become reunited her with her kittens.

As I watched her walking into the trap, I wondered, could someone have told my mother where Maggie and I ended up? Was it possible that somehow she had learned we were well taken care of? The animal world has a mysterious way of spreading information. It hadn't occurred to me until just this moment, but perhaps my family had seen my picture in the ads for the pet store. They still run that picture of me from when I was a little kitten. Surely Oliver, Smokey or my dad had seen it by now and recognized me!

A new image of mother at peace began to supersede the haunting memory of her crying out for us that fateful day. At last, I was filled with a tranquil serenity when thinking of mother, instead of heartache. Perhaps, just maybe, I would be able to fall asleep tonight without needing my own foot to pacify me.